SPRING
DAWN

SPRING DAWN

Seasons of Faith, Book 3

Rebekah Lyn

Other Books by Rebekah Lyn

Seasons of Faith
Summer Storms
Winter's End
Spring Dawn
Christmas Vow *coming soon*

Coastal Chronicles
Julianne
Jessie

April 2005

CHAPTER ONE

Stephen fumbled the phone into its cradle and leaned back in his chair. What had he just agreed to? He'd had no idea stopping a corporate coup for one of the hotel's newest clients would draw so much attention to him.

A shadow fell over the desk and he felt a hand on his shoulder. He looked up, his brown eyes meeting the quizzical blue ones of his boss and friend, Lizzie Reynolds.

"Did you hear me?" She studied him, one eyebrow arched.

"What?" Stephen shook his head to clear his rushing thoughts.

Lizzie ran a hand through her rumpled blond curls in a failed attempt to calm them. "I asked if you were going to be at the Concierge Club dinner Tuesday."

"Oh. Yeah, I'll be there." He'd forgotten about it, but knew he didn't have any other plans. "Cafe Marie at six, right?"

Lizzie nodded. "I can't wait to hear what everyone is planning for Bacchus Bash."

"What is that again?"

"You've never been?" Lizzie cried.

"I don't think so."

"It's a charity event put on by the Central Florida Hotel and Lodging Association to raise funds for hospitality schools in the area. There are food booths sponsored by hotels and restaurants, entertainment, and a silent auction. You never know who you will run into. Last year I saw a singer from a popular boy band," Lizzie blushed, "not that I knew who he was, but Stephanie recognized him."

"Sounds like fun. When is it?"

"The second Friday of April."

"That's next week."

Lizzie glanced at the desk calendar. "I guess it is. Time has flown by since I returned from Vermont."

"Seems like you've been living here since your trip," Stephen said.

Lizzie shrugged and indulged herself in a slow neck roll. "There's been a lot to do between the Spring Break rush and the boom in our summer wedding reservations. Tammy needs to hire someone to help with groups and weddings."

"Maybe when Mr. Kingsley finalizes the deal to buy out Ryland Resorts," Stephen stopped when he saw the surprised look on Lizzie's face.

"What do you know about that?"

"Nothing," Stephen sputtered, "just the rumors."

"No, you know something else." Lizzie leaned over, placed her elbows on the desk and rested her chin on her hands. "Spill."

"I don't know much. Mr. Kingsley is running backgrounds on everyone working for Ryland and asked me to review a few people he had some concerns about."

Lizzie's elbows slipped, her chin having a near miss with the desk. "He asked you to what?"

"To, to…"

"I heard you, I just can't believe it."

"Me either," Stephen admitted. "He said he was impressed with my instincts and resourcefulness."

"When was this?"

Stephen pointed to the phone. "A few minutes ago, before you came over."

"That explains why you looked so preoccupied. Is this about that business in February with the Silken Pleasures corporate group?"

"I should have minded my own business."

"You saved Mrs. Therriault from losing her company and your actions secured her business here for the next three years."

"The signs were all there. Mrs. Therriault admitted to her assistant she would have seen them herself if Mrs. Cartwright hadn't cozied up to her and lulled her into a sense of camaraderie. It was dumb luck on my part. I don't know how I'm supposed to investigate these people for Mr. Kingsley. What if I screw up?"

"He was right, you do have good instincts and you have a way of seeing through the facades people put on. You'll do fine."

"I'm glad you're so sure. I don't want to lose this job. I'm kind of starting to enjoy it."

Lizzie laughed. "Well, we can't have you losing a job you kind of like. I'll help you out any way I can."

Stephen stood and brushed at some lint on his pants. "No reason worrying until I get more information from Mr. Kingsley. Right now I believe it's time to make my rounds in the concierge lounge."

"Anyone exciting staying with us? I haven't had a chance to review the guest manifest this morning."

"None of the regulars are in this week. The hotel is at sixty percent occupancy with only twenty percent in concierge. Kind of a nice lull." Stephen grinned.

"You can say that again. Memorial Day will be here before we know it and the summer crowds will descend. I'm going to catch up on some paperwork. Pop into my office after your rounds." Lizzie gave Stephen a pat on the shoulder before disappearing into a tiny office.

CHAPTER TWO

Lizzie dropped down into the stiff office chair and rubbed her eyes before turning to her computer. She clicked through the accumulation of email, stopping her cursor when she came to the last message. Ian never emailed her at work. He respected her wish to keep her work and personal lives separate. Why would he email her now?

She opened a desk drawer and pulled out her cell phone. Had Ian sent a text? If it was an emergency, he would have called or texted. Why an email? Her gaze wandered out into the main room of the front office. Two room assignment staff sat at desks, reviewing reservations, putting together the puzzle that would maximize use of the hotel's available rooms.

Lizzie returned her attention to the computer. The subject line of the email read "Quick Question". She clicked it and waited for the message to open. She scanned it twice, then moved the cursor to the delete icon. Her finger hovered over the mouse for several seconds before she clicked delete. She knew deleting the message without responding wasn't the answer to her problem, but it was the only option she had at that moment, the only way to put off seeing him and falling deeper into a web of desire and despair. Tomorrow, she would talk to him tomorrow.

Her eyes burned and she blinked several times until the words on the computer screen came into focus. The hotel may be quiet today, but there were always reports to complete and forecasts to review. Pushing aside thoughts of Ian, she opened a spreadsheet and buried herself in work.

A knock on the doorframe startled her. She looked up as Stephen sauntered in.

"Why don't you take a break and have lunch with me?"

"It's not time yet, is it?"

"Look at your watch, Lizzie, dear. It's almost two o'clock."

Lizzie did check her watch. "How is that possible? Why didn't you come by after morning rounds?"

"I did, but you were so engrossed in your work I didn't want to disturb you. Now you need to take a break before you go cross-eyed." Stephen reached out a hand to Lizzie. When she stood, her knees and ankles popped, and she swayed for a moment.

"I'm getting old, Stephen."

"Nonsense. You do spend too much time behind this desk, though. You should come out on rounds more often."

Lizzie thought about that and agreed; she did need to get out more. She missed interacting with the guests; hearing their stories energized her. Her promotion to manager of Guest Services and Concierge, six months earlier, found her torn between her responsibilities to the employees and the guests.

"I wish I could," she said, following Stephen out of the office into a side hall that led to the hotel lobby.

"So, come with me after lunch. We'll check the stock in the concierge lounge for this evening's cocktail hour. Maybe you could even come up for a few minutes before you leave tonight. There is a couple that hasn't missed the cocktails all week and I think you'd enjoy meeting them."

It sounded like a splendid idea, but she didn't want to commit, knowing how much work she still had to get done. "I'll try to make it if I can finish before the hour is up."

Lizzie could feel Stephen's disappointment even though he didn't say a word. As they passed through the lobby, Lizzie scanned the faces of the guests loitering in armchairs. Her gaze moved to the floral arrangements, taking note of two that were starting to wilt, and then to the large windows looking out across the street to Lake Eola. A fine coat of pollen lay over the windows that had shined yesterday.

"Stop it," Stephen hissed as he pulled open a door that led them to a service corridor.

"What?"

"Stop taking inventory of the hotel."

Lizzie came to a halt and stared at Stephen.

"You do it every time you leave the office. You've even started doing it at the Concierge Club dinners."

"What do you mean?"

"Your eyes move around a room, taking notes on the details that need correction. You know we are going to Cafe Marie because the owner of the Bread Basket asked us not to bring you back. Last month you pointed out fifteen minor maintenance issues before we even received our appetizers."

"No I didn't," Lizzie objected, aghast.

Stephen slipped an arm around her shoulders and walked them on. "I can understand why you might be hyper-vigilant. You've had a lot going on." Stephen ticked them off on his fingers. "All the hurricanes last summer, then that guy who was stalking you, and last month a snowstorm left you stranded, not to mention your promotion. Maybe it's time you talked to someone about it."

Stephen paused before the door to the staff cafeteria. "How are things with you and Ian?"

"Things are fine. We've both been busy, of course, but other than that fine." Lizzie reached for the door, but Stephen touched her arm.

"You know you can talk to me, right? Anytime."

The concern in Stephen's eyes reached right into Lizzie's soul. "Of course I know that. You've become one of my best friends, but everything is fine. I promise." She smiled and squeezed his hand. "Now what's for lunch? I just realized I'm starving."

CHAPTER THREE

Manicured grass cushioned the steps of the four men as they clambered out of two golf carts toward the seventh tee. Jeffrey placed his ball on the pin and squinted, his sunglasses no match for the light reflecting off the glass-like surface of the lake. The men with him grew quiet while Jeffrey lined up his shot. He waited for the gentle breeze to still, then swung. His club connected with a sharp thwack, sending the ball sailing across the narrow lake and onto the green.

"Not bad, Robbins," one of the men congratulated Jeffrey before taking his own spot at the tee.

"Pure luck, sir," Jeffrey said. The endless rounds of golf with the executives behind the construction of The Plaza were growing old. He'd learned how to condense his information into bullet points and give a project update between holes. By the fifth most of the executives had lost interest in the update completely and Jeffrey had to fight to keep them on task.

"No, your game has definitely improved since we started these meetings last year." The man pulled several clubs from his bag before settling on one and moving into position. Jeffrey bit back his frustration, waiting for the rest of the party to complete their shots.

"As I was saying, we are on target for completion of the..."

"Jeffrey, relax," one of the men said. "You did a fine job of making up time when the hurricanes came through last summer. The cost overruns have been minimal, well within what we expected. Enjoy this beautiful day."

"With all due respect, sir, if we aren't going to talk about the project, I would be more comfortable returning to the site."

The men were taking their seats on the golf carts, leaving Jeffrey standing alone. The driver pulled a stick of gum from his shirt pocket, peeled back the wrapper, and folded the gum in half before placing it between his front teeth. He chewed for several seconds before responding.

"Sure, Robbins, we can drop you off at the ninth hole, it's close to the clubhouse."

"Thank you, sir." Jeffrey took the remaining seat on the golf cart and resigned himself to finishing two more holes.

Thirty minutes later, Jeffrey hopped off the cart, collected his golf bag, and watched the men drive away. He looked toward the back patio of the clubhouse, where several patrons were enjoying a late lunch. He shifted the golf bag on his shoulder and walked across the green expanse.

"Good afternoon, sir, would you like a table?" a server greeted Jeffrey as he reached the patio.

"No, thank you. I'm just passing through." Jeffrey reached the door to the restaurant and maneuvered through the tables, trying not to knock anyone with his golf bag. He went out into the sunshine and found his truck.

Before starting the engine, he checked his cell phone and found he'd missed three calls. The first two were from his office, but the third was from Ian.

He and Ian had been good friends years ago, but had fallen out of touch after Jeffrey's fiancée, Camylle, had died. Working together last summer to restore Lizzie's house had drawn them together again, but Jeffrey still wasn't entirely comfortable around Ian. He dialed his office, starting his truck as the phone rang.

"Hollisbrook Construction, this is Jenny."

"It's Jeffrey. I'm on my way back. What did I miss?"

"I didn't expect you back today."

"Change of plans." Jeffrey tucked the phone between his ear and shoulder while he backed out of the parking spot and circled the lot to the main entrance. He could hear Jenny shuffling papers.

"We could use you back here. The plumbing contractor hasn't returned my call and we have another inspection coming up next week."

Jeffrey let out a loud breath. "Can you connect me to their office?"

"Sure, hang on."

Jeffrey soon heard ringing and was merging onto Interstate-4 when the line was answered.

"This is Jeffrey Robbins with Hollisbrook Construction calling for Gregory."

"I'm sorry, Mr. Robbins, he is out of the office. May I take a message?" the receptionist asked.

"Your team is behind schedule and Gregory isn't returning our calls."

"I can tell him you called when he returns."

"When do you think that will be?"

"I can't say for sure. He may be out until the morning."

Jeffrey's grip on the steering wheel tightened. "Why don't you track him down and tell him if I don't hear from him by five today I will be finding another contractor."

The receptionist's tone changed from cool but pleasant to worried. "I'm not sure I can do that, Mr. Robbins."

"I'm sure you can find a way." Jeffrey disconnected the call and guided his truck down the off ramp, coasting to a stop at a red light. Five minutes later, he stepped into the trailer used as an office on the construction site.

"Any luck?" Jenny asked.

Jeffrey shook his head. "Do we have the paperwork here on the plumbing bids?"

"I think that is all in the main office. You want me to call to see if they can send it over?"

"Just get me the information on the two bids closest to Gregory's. If he doesn't call today, we're moving on."

Jenny was dialing before Jeffrey left the trailer again, crossing the dusty expanse to the growing tower.

CHAPTER FOUR

Ian gazed out the window, the setting sun painting the sky a pale orange, the tall pines fading to dark silhouettes. He bounced the end of his pencil on the desk, the rhythmic tapping the only sound in the office. He'd spent most of the day looking out the window, unable to focus.

"Is there anything else you need before I leave?"

Ian turned to see his secretary, a thin woman in her fifties, leaning against the doorframe. "No thanks, Sheila."

"Don't stay too late," she admonished with a smile.

"If I don't get these plans done soon, I'm going to end up working over the weekend."

"You were daydreaming again, weren't you?" Sheila stepped into the office and placed her hands on the back of one of the chairs across from Ian's desk. "When are you going to ask her to marry you?"

"If only it was that easy. I was sure the right time would come while we were in Vermont, but there is so much she still needs to sort out for herself."

"There won't ever be a perfect time."

"I'm beginning to understand that. I don't want her to feel pressured, though, and I don't want to scare her away. We were in a good place when we came home, but the last couple of weeks we've barely spoken."

Sheila stepped forward and took a seat in the chair. "That explains why you've been so irritable."

"Have I? I'm sorry, Sheila."

She patted his hand. "I knew something had to be bothering you. Have you been praying about this?"

Ian thought for a minute. "I don't know if I've been praying for the right things."

"It can be hard to know what to pray. Ask God for his guidance and wisdom. He will let you know when Lizzie is ready."

"I know you're right. I need to be patient, but I want to start our life together now."

"I hope she knows how lucky she is to have found you."

"I'm pretty lucky myself."

"You should call her, take her out to dinner tonight. Maybe if you see her you will be able to focus on finishing the plans."

Ian glanced at the clock and then the phone. "Maybe I will."

Sheila stood. "I'll see you tomorrow."

When he heard the outer-office door close, Ian reached for the phone.

"Hey, it's Lizzie. Leave me a message."

Ian hung up without leaving one. He pushed back his chair and wandered past Sheila's desk, down a hall to a small kitchen. He pulled a bottle of water from the refrigerator and took a long drink. He wanted to rush out the door, sweep Lizzie out of her office, and take her to a quiet dinner. Instead, he tossed the empty bottle in a recycling bin and returned to his office. With a last look out the now dark window, he seated himself at his drafting table and started sketching.

CHAPTER FIVE

"Good night." Michelle waved at her friends as they parted in the parking garage. Country, rap, pop, and classical music blasted from the stream of cars slithering down from the upper levels of the garage and she happily added her own rock-and-roll to the soundtrack when she started her car. Most of the cars were turning right, toward I-4. She turned left, toward Lake Eola, grumbling as she seemed to catch every traffic light.

When she finally arrived at her destination, she found the parking lot near capacity, snagging a spot as another car pulled out. She checked her hair and lipstick in the mirror before hurrying across the lot to the restaurant entrance. A party of five entered before her and she scanned the waiting crowd. Jeffrey waved from the bar and stood to greet her.

"Sorry I'm late," Michelle said.

"Traffic is a bear this time of day," Jeffrey said. "Would you like something to drink? It's going to be about fifteen minutes before a table is ready."

Michelle noticed Jeffrey had what looked like a soda in front of him. "Would you mind if I had a glass of wine?"

"Not at all." Jeffrey waved to the bar tender and Michelle ordered a glass of house red. "Rough day?"

"Not really, just a lot of projects going on."

"I understand that. I'm having an issue with one of my contractors. Tomorrow I have to let him go and hire someone else."

"That doesn't sound good."

Jeffrey shrugged. "Part of the business. It's the first time I've had to deal with this myself, so I hope it doesn't get too crazy."

"Robbins, table for two?" a server called out as he wandered around the entry area.

Jeffrey stood and waved. They followed the server through the crowded restaurant to a table on the patio.

"It's a beautiful evening, I'm glad you asked to sit outside," Michelle said as the server motioned to a chair.

The sun was setting behind the downtown skyscrapers, casting an orange glow on the walls of glass. A soft breeze played with Michelle's hair, which tickled her ears. The smell of fried foods mixed with the camellia blossoms surrounding the patio.

"How is the search for a new keyboard player going?" Jeffrey asked.

"We've had several people contact us. Matt and I are meeting with them this weekend. I'm glad Jonesy decided to stick with us when Tina bailed. It would be a pain to have to find a new guitar player too."

"Seems like people would be lining up to join after the big shows you've been landing."

Michelle held back the smile that tugged at her lips. Her band, *Tangled Web*, had gotten a big break six weeks earlier when they were asked to open for the hot, new group Wonderland. That had been one of the best nights of her life, but when she went to work the next day, she found the body of Amanda Barnes, one of her coworkers, in the office bathroom. The discovery had naturally cast a shadow over Michelle's excitement.

In a macabre twist, when the news mentioned Amanda had been at the concert before her death, the band's popularity skyrocketed. Part of Michelle felt bad that she was benefitting from Amanda's death.

"Things have been going well lately." Michelle reached for her wine glass and took a sip. "Sometimes I still wonder if there was something I could have done to prevent Amanda's death, though."

"You can't think like that. You were still on stage when she left."

Jeffrey's words held tenderness, but Michelle didn't dare look into his eyes. Instead, she looked across the parking lot toward a quiet side street.

A server arrived at the table and placed a basket of bread between them, and took their orders. Michelle reached for a piece of bread and slathered it with butter.

"Have you read through the pamphlet I gave you?"

Michelle nodded then took a bite of bread, hoping Jeffrey would let the subject drop.

"Did it help answer any of your questions?"

She wasn't about to admit she'd read the pamphlet "You're Saved, Now What" two or three times a week since he'd given it to her. If anything she had more questions than before. When Jeffrey had told her he'd given his life to Christ, she'd been skeptical. They'd tried dating in the past, and he'd turned out to be a jerk. Since Amanda's death they'd met for lunch or dinner a few times and he called at least once a week. She didn't think they were dating, but she was beginning to wish they were.

"Sure, I guess I get it," she said before shoving the rest of her bread into her mouth.

Jeffrey chuckled and Michelle knew she must look like a squirrel packing away nuts for the winter. "It's okay if you don't understand. It took me years to believe any of it, and when I did, I felt guilty I hadn't come to accept the truth of God's love sooner, that I had let..." Jeffrey looked away.

Michelle remembered the night he'd told her about his new-found faith, how his fiancée, Camylle, had tried to get him to accept God before she died. "Camylle would be happy to know you came around," she whispered.

Jeffrey returned his gaze to Michelle and nodded. She thought she saw tears in his eyes, but he blinked and they were gone. "Lizzie explained to me that when the seeds of God's love are planted in us, sometimes they take a long time to take root and grow, and sometimes they seem to blossom overnight. I can't do anything to make you believe, but I owe it to you to provide the support and attention that might help those seeds grow."

Michelle studied Jeffrey; his brown eyes were kind, not the angry rocks she'd seen in him last summer. His whole face seemed softer, more relaxed, and she realized he'd looked this way every time she'd seen him since Amanda's death.

"I told you before, I'm happy to answer any questions you have, and Lizzie would be happy to meet with you. She's even asked a couple of times when I'm going to introduce the two of you. I think you'd like her."

"So, are you two dating now?" Michelle found herself dreading the answer.

Jeffrey shook his head. "She's dating someone else and I have a feeling they'll be getting married soon. I'm not sure why they aren't engaged already."

"Are you okay with that? I got the impression you were interested in her."

"Ian's a good guy and he would do anything for her. There was a time when I thought maybe I had a chance, but," Jeffrey shrugged, "it all worked out for the best."

Their food arrived and they spent the next several minutes in silence. Michelle was embarrassed by the flutter of hope she'd felt when she learned Lizzie was involved with someone else.

"We're playing at the Social again this weekend," Michelle said as the waiter cleared the empty plates. "I can have a ticket at the door for you if you want to come."

"Sure, that sounds like fun."

Jeffrey walked her to her car and gave her a hug. He smelled like fresh cut grass and sawdust. His breath on her neck was warm and she turned her face to his, but he released her and stepped back. "I'll see you Saturday."

Jeffrey took a few steps toward the rear of the car, stopped, then waved and continued on.

CHAPTER SIX

Tinkling metal and glass from a wind chime drifted on a cool breeze. Along the narrow path to the front steps, last week's tender green sprouts now stood two inches high. Lizzie smiled at the thought of the vibrant blossoms these sprouts promised to yield in a few more weeks. She was looking forward to her first spring in her new home, anxious to discover what plants may have gone unrecognized.

The front porch light provided a welcoming glow in the lengthening shadows of twilight. Lizzie unlocked the door and stepped inside, her cell phone vibrating as she closed the door behind her. She pulled the phone from her pocket and found a text message from Jeffrey. Hey. Haven't heard from you in a few days. Hope things are good.

Her finger hesitated over the delete option before moving to reply. *I'm fine, just been busy. You?*

Less than a minute passed before his reply came. *Mostly good. You free for lunch this weekend?*

Lizzie walked into the kitchen, setting her purse and phone on the counter while she poured herself a glass of tea. She gulped down half the glass before reaching for the phone again. *Sure. Saturday around 12:30?*

Sounds good. Priano's in Winter Park?

Lizzie keyed in her acceptance, returned the phone to the counter, and pulled a stack of mail from her purse. She settled herself in the living room, savoring the silence of her home. She flipped through the assortment of credit card offers and advertisements, removing the application forms for shredding. The last envelope, though, caught her attention. The return address was vaguely familiar, written in a confident script. She searched through her memories trying to place the address in Massachusetts, but couldn't pin it down. She slipped her letter opener under the flap and sliced through the paper in one smooth motion. There was a single page inside, handwritten rather than typed. She scanned the letter twice before letting it flutter to the ground.

Her gaze moved to three photos hanging on the living room wall. While cleaning the walls in preparation for painting, she'd uncovered three drawings, most likely done by a child. Loathe to destroy them, she had taken photos and hung the prints in the dining room. Later she'd learned that the current owner's mother had done the drawings as a child. Lizzie hadn't heard from him in months, not since the police had arrested his stepson for stalking and assaulting her. She picked up the letter again.

Dear Ms. Reynolds,

I hope you are doing well. My agent, Mr. Rosenbloom, tells me you are maintaining the house quite well. I suspect the neighbors are grateful for your intervention. My wife, Melinda, and I will be in Florida in a few weeks and we would like to stop by to see you. I'll be honest; she wasn't too keen to meet you at first. Ralph's actions were shocking and an embarrassment for her. Once I showed her the photos you gave me of mother's art, she agreed to a short visit. We wouldn't want to impose. I know you are busy with your work. I believe you have my phone number, but just in case, you can reach me at 617-555-3479. I look forward to hearing from you.

Regards,
Jacob Phillips

Why would Mrs. Phillips want to see the house? Was she planning on taking it away from Lizzie? The thought of Ralph Anderson made Lizzie's stomach clench. It had been seven months since Mr. Anderson had shown up on the front porch of Lizzie's neighbor, Mae, asking questions. Mr. Anderson suspected his stepfather of having an affair after discovering a check made out to Lizzie. Her efforts to explain that the money was reimbursement for damage the house sustained during Hurricane Charley were in vain. She'd never met Jacob Phillips, but Ralph didn't believe her.

If Ian hadn't shown up when he did, Lizzie couldn't bear the thought of what might have happened. It had taken weeks for the nightmares to stop.

Ian would be over in a heartbeat if she called. She longed to hide herself away in his strong arms and she reached for the phone again. Instead of dialing, she shoved the phone into her pocket, scooped up her keys, and left the house.

CHAPTER SEVEN

In less than a minute, Lizzie stood on her neighbor's front porch, raising her hand to knock. The door opened before her knuckles hit the wood. She just missed the forehead of a slender man with a long, narrow face.

"Good evening, Lizzie. How are you?" The man stepped back, allowing Lizzie to enter the room.

"I'm fine, Liam. How are you?" Lizzie looked around the tidy living room. "Is your mother all right?"

Liam chuckled. "Mother is fine. She's in the bathroom, washing a stain out of her shirt. We went to dinner and a waiter spilled a glass of wine on her. Come on in and have a seat."

"If she's busy, I can see her tomorrow." Lizzie stepped back to the door.

"Why would you come back tomorrow when you're here now?" Mae stepped out of the bathroom, drying her hands on a towel.

The white-haired lady wore a pair of crisp navy blue slacks, and a baggy Miami Dolphins T-shirt. Lizzie suppressed a smile at the sight. She'd never seen Mae in anything less than a button down blouse.

"You didn't think I owned any T-shirts, did you?" Mae asked.

"I didn't." Lizzie giggled.

"Don't let her fool you," Liam cut in. "That's one of Avery's old shirts."

"Now why'd you have to go and tell her that?" Mae chided Liam.

"That makes me feel better. I was beginning to think you had a whole secret life I didn't know about."

Mae gave Lizzie a grin and winked at Liam. "How do you know I don't?"

"Mother." Liam gave an exasperated sigh.

"Oh, you go on home. Sarah is going to be wondering what happened to you." Mae waved off her son. "Come on and sit down, Lizzie. Can I get you something to drink?"

"No, thank you."

Liam stepped over to his mother and gave her a kiss on the cheek. "Good night. I had a nice time."

"Good night, sweetheart. I love you."

"Good to see you, Lizzie," Liam called as he stepped outside.

"He's a good boy," Mae said as she took a seat in a rocking chair across from Lizzie.

"You are lucky to have such adoring sons," Lizzie said, happy to know her elderly neighbor was so well looked after.

"That I am. I know some women who have been practically abandoned by their children." Mae glanced out the window to Lizzie's home. "That Mary who used to live in your place is a prime example."

"Funny you should mention her. That's why I came over."

"She hasn't started haunting you, has she?" Mae laughed.

"Not exactly, but I received a letter from her son. You know I'm still renting the house from him and it seems he wants to bring his wife by in a few weeks."

"The woman who raised that rotten Ralph Anderson?" Mae's face crinkled in distaste. "I'd like to give her a piece of my mind."

Lizzie knew her friend would do just that given the chance and maybe it wouldn't be such a bad thing.

"I'm worried they will want me to move out," Lizzie confessed. Speaking the words to someone else helped lift the weight off her heart.

"Why would they want that? You've turned that old wreck into a beautiful home. Everyone in the neighborhood is grateful for all the work you've done. Emma Jean, down the street, was telling me the value of her property has gone up nearly ten thousand dollars since you finished renovating."

Lizzie felt a glow of pride that faded quickly. Had her property increase provided Mr. Phillips with an incentive to try to sell now?

"When is Mr. Phillips planning to visit?"

"His letter said a few weeks. I'm supposed to call and let him know when I am available."

"You let me know when he plans to visit and I'll make sure I'm home. You should have Ian with you as well, so the Phillips can see what a nice couple you are." Mae's eyes twinkled. "I suspect the two of you will be starting a family there soon."

Lizzie felt her face flush. "We've only been dating a few months."

"Sometimes a few months is all it takes, and I've seen the way you look at each other."

Lizzie tensed. Could Mae see the tension Lizzie felt when she was close to Ian? She dared a look at her neighbor and found Mae's face had clouded.

"Come to think of it, I haven't seen Ian at your house in the past couple of weeks. Is he out of town?"

"No, we've just had crazy schedules. You know how busy this town gets during Spring Break and he's designing a new shopping center."

Mae nodded, but her smile didn't return. "I'm sure things will be fine when Mr. and Mrs. Phillips visit, but I will keep it in my prayers."

"Thank you, Mae. That means a lot to me." Lizzie glanced out the window. Night had fallen and street lamps were all that illuminated the quiet street. Lizzie stood. "I should go home. Early day tomorrow."

Mae rose and pulled Lizzie into a hug. "Don't work too hard."

Lizzie stopped at the end of the walkway and looked back. Mae stood in the doorway and waved. Lizzie returned the gesture, knowing her friend would watch over her until her own front door closed. She jogged across the street and raised her hand in a final greeting before stepping inside.

CHAPTER EIGHT

"Mr. Cavanaugh?" a woman's voice whispered, rousing Ian from a deep sleep.

"What?" he croaked, lifting his head and looking around. Something stuck to his cheek and he brushed at it, realizing it was a piece of paper. The outline of his desk and the bookcase by the door confirmed his dismay; he was in his office.

"Did you stay here all night?" Sheila asked.

"I must have fallen asleep." Ian slipped off the drafting table stool and raised his arms over his head, his back cracking several times as he stretched.

Sheila's pursed lips and narrowed eyes alerted him to her disapproval. "I'll make some coffee." She turned on her heel and left the office before Ian could speak.

Ian stepped into the small bathroom attached to his office. When he saw his reflection in the mirror, he understood Sheila's disapproval. Matted hair clung to one side of his face above an angry red stain on his cheek. His shirt was a mess of crisscrossing wrinkles and dark circles rimmed his eyes. He opened the cabinet underneath the sink and set to work.

By the time Sheila returned with two cups of coffee he had brushed his teeth, combed his hair, and shaved. His pants were in the same shape as his shirt, but his dry cleaning would be delivered in a few hours and he could change then.

"I thought you were going to take Lizzie out to dinner last night," Sheila said as she set a cup of coffee on his desk.

"She didn't answer when I called." Ian took a long sip of the hot liquid, grateful Sheila enjoyed strong coffee.

Sheila wandered to the drafting table and shifted around some papers. "This is beautiful, but it doesn't look like a shopping center." She held up a large sheet with a drawing of a sprawling Italian-style villa.

Ian shrugged. "I got distracted. The shopping center plan is underneath."

Sheila shuffled the pages again, pulling out an even larger sheet and studying it for several minutes. "Not bad. When are you presenting it to the builder?"

"We have a meeting Monday afternoon."

"Good, that gives you time to fine tune it."

"What do you mean?" Ian set down his coffee cup and moved to the drafting table, taking the architectural plan from Sheila.

The secretary pointed to a spot where Ian had drawn a fountain with traffic routed around it. "That is going to do nothing but cause trouble. People won't be paying attention, there will be wrecks everyday." She pointed to a large mark on the plan. "This is going to be an anchor store, right? You can't take up prime parking space with that much landscaping."

"But it softens the look of the place."

Sheila shook her head. "No one really cares how nice a shopping center looks, they only care about convenience. If you want to make it pretty, add hanging baskets along the walkways or turn the support beams into planters. Don't impede walkways or take up parking space."

Ian sighed. Commercial real estate projects were becoming less enjoyable, but that was where the money was these days. The residents of Orlando seemed content with neighborhoods that looked identical, the color of your front door the only way you knew you were returning to the right house.

There were exceptions, of course, in some of the more exclusive areas where celebrities built their mansions. Unfortunately, those people weren't interested in a small design firm they'd never heard of. He needed a project to make a name for himself, until then he had to settle for shopping centers and office complexes.

"Do you want me to run over to the bakery and get you something for breakfast?"

"If they still have a spinach and egg soufflé that would be good, if not an everything bagel with cream cheese is fine," Ian replied.

"I'll be back in a few minutes."

When Sheila had gone, Ian picked up the sketch and studied it again. She'd made some good points about traffic flow. With the stores the developer had contracted so far, this was likely to be a busy place, especially at Christmas. He unrolled a new page and sat down to start over. As he drew he imagined Lizzie shopping here; what would she like to see?

"Sorry it took so long. There was a line and only one person ringing people up." Ian's stomach growled as soon as he smelled the soufflé Sheila carried. He glanced at the clock, surprised to see half an hour had passed since she had left.

"Thank you, Sheila. I don't know what I'd do without you." Ian kissed her on the cheek as he took the food.

"Maybe if you didn't have me to rely on you'd get off your duff and get married," Sheila teased.

Ian sat down and dug into his food, ignoring her remark.

"I'll be at my desk if you need anything," Sheila said, pulling the office door closed behind her.

Ian scarfed down the food and finished his coffee before turning to his computer and checking his email. He zeroed in on a message from Lizzie sent the previous evening.

Sorry I missed you today. There was so much to catch up on. Our counts are lower next week so I should have some breathing room. Maybe we can have dinner this weekend.

Love you,
Lizzie

Ian checked the time of the email. Nine fifteen. Late enough to be sure he wouldn't call her, and now, if he responded to her home email, she wouldn't receive the message until after work. Why was she making things so difficult? He tapped a fingernail on the computer keyboard before sending a reply and then setting a reminder to text her at lunchtime. Maybe she wouldn't be annoyed with his text if it came during lunch.

He stood, collected his coffee cup and made his way into the kitchen. Half a pot of coffee remained and he poured himself a fresh cup, spooning in a touch of sugar. "Will you help me remember to make a dinner reservation?" he asked as he passed Sheila's desk.

"Why don't I just do that for you now? Where do you want to go?"

Ian stopped at his office door. "I don't know yet. Is any place open to take reservations this early?"

"There's a new place on Sand Lake, they're open for lunch, and I know the chef." Sheila grinned. "What time?"

"Seven should give Lizzie time to go home, get changed, and have a buffer for whatever emergency comes up to keep her late." Ian heard the bitterness in his last words and wished he could take them back.

"It takes a while to get used to being in a management position and I'm sure there is some anxiety about the changes coming with the big merger."

"What merger?" Ian moved closer to Sheila's desk.

"She hasn't told you? Mr. Kingsley, the owner of Hotel Lago, is buying out Ryland Resorts. Another four resorts will be added to the Kingsley portfolio."

"How did you hear this?"

"I have friends. One of them works in Mr. Kingsley's corporate office. She's been hearing rumors since February, but the paperwork was finalized last week. Lizzie really hasn't told you anything about it?"

Ian shook his head. "Maybe she didn't know. If the sale was just finalized..."

"Maybe, but surely she heard rumors. News like that is hard to keep quiet."

"I guess we have a lot to catch up on over dinner."

"I'll write down the name of the restaurant and some directions for you once I get it all set."

"Thanks, Sheila." Ian stepped back into his office and settled at the drafting table, wondering what else Lizzie had forgotten to tell him about.

CHAPTER NINE

A knock on the door interrupted Lizzie. "Come in," she called as she saved the spreadsheet she was working on.

Stephen pushed open the door and stepped in. Lizzie noticed his furrowed brow and pushed aside the mind-numbing reports she'd been working on all morning.

"I hate to bother you, but do you have a few minutes?"

"Of course. I could use a break from this anyway." Lizzie waved at the computer then motioned for Stephen to take the chair on the other side of the desk "What's wrong?"

"Mr. Kingsley emailed me the first list of employees he wants me to review."

"That was fast. How many are on the list?"

"Only five. He said he wanted to go through each property individually. These are all at a resort in Colorado."

"That doesn't sound too bad."

Stephen shook his head. "I didn't think he was serious. What if I get it wrong and they lose their job because of me?"

"You said Mr. Kingsley is running background checks on everyone. Did he give you any reason for sending these names?"

"Only that they were the newest employees with the resort."

"Do you want me to contact HR and see what they found on them, maybe get a copy of their résumés?"

Stephen removed his glasses, pulled a cloth from his pocket, and polished the lenses. Lizzie had learned this was the way he bought himself time to think and leaned back in her chair, content to wait.

"A copy of their résumés might give me an idea what is causing Mr. Kingsley concern. Maybe they don't have much work history."

Lizzie nodded. "I'll see what I can find out. It's been too long since Cynthia and I talked anyway."

Stephen stood. "I appreciate it."

As the door closed, Lizzie picked up the phone and dialed; trying to remember the last time she'd seen her friend Cynthia Bigelow. Cynthia had been the assistant to the general manager at one of the Disney resorts Lizzie had worked at several years before. The two had become friends after Lizzie brought a particular guest to the attention of the general manager.

Marvin Pinick stayed at the resort every four to five months. He bombarded the staff with minor complaints, always leaving with at least one night refunded to him. Sometimes more. When Lizzie found out Marvin had a history of similar behavior at other resorts in town, and had even been banned from one, she decided it was time to talk to management.

The front desk manager didn't seem to care and told her to keep her focus on checking in guests and not worry about the running of the hotel. Lizzie had steamed about the lack of concern until Marvin returned again and ended up with his entire stay refunded by the hotel. That's when Lizzie had stalked upstairs to the main operations office and met Cynthia.

Cynthia took her job as a gatekeeper for the general manager seriously, and had given Lizzie a stern look. When Lizzie explained what had been happening every time Marvin stayed, Cynthia's face had softened and she'd arranged for Lizzie to meet the general manager.

"Hello?" The voice on the other end of the phone interrupted Lizzie's reminiscing.

"Cynthia, it's Lizzie. How are you?"

"Lizzie, it's been ages. I'm good, how are you? I heard about your promotion, congratulations."

"Thanks. It hasn't been quite what I expected, but I'm getting used to it."

Cynthia laughed. "You never knew there could be so much paperwork did you?"

Lizzie sighed. "Is it true Mr. Kingsley is close to finalizing the deal to buy out Ryland Resorts?"

"The deal went through last week. You haven't received anything about it yet?"

"No, the only reason I knew it was close was because Mr. Kingsley asked one of my employees to review a few of the Ryland employees."

"You mean Stephen," Cynthia stated. "I thought that was a little odd."

Lizzie sat up straighter, surprised her friend knew about the unusual request. "How do you know about Stephen?"

"Mr. Kingsley told me to help him out if he had any questions."

"That's why I'm calling. Stephen received five names today that Mr. Kingsley wants him to look into."

"The last five to be hired."

"That's right. Were you blind copied on the email from Mr. Kingsley?"

"You should be doing the detective work for Mr. K. He wanted to keep me in the loop since I'm working with the company running the background checks, but didn't want Stephen to think I was going to interfere in his work."

"I'll leave the detecting to Stephen, I've enough on my own plate already. I'm glad to know you're the one keeping up with the background checks, though. I think you and Stephen will get along well."

"I hope we get to meet before this is over. The story of his work with the Silken Pleasures group and the plot he uncovered is well known here in the office. I'll send him the résumés and a few other things he might find helpful."

"Thanks. I know he'll appreciate it."

"Happy to help. Tell him to give me a call if he has any questions."

"I will. You and I need to have lunch sometime soon."

"I would love that. I'll check my calendar and send you a note."

"I look forward to it."

CHAPTER TEN

Lizzie hung up, pushed back from her desk, straightened her skirt, and stepped out of the office. She found Stephen at his desk, staring at a website she didn't recognize. "I spoke with my friend Cynthia and she's going to email you the résumés."

Stephen toggled over to his email program. "That was fast," he said as he clicked on a new message. "How did she know who I was looking for?"

"Mr. Kingsley told her you were doing some work for him and she should give you any help you needed. He must have given her the names too." Lizzie felt bad about the half-truth, but didn't want to shake Stephen's confidence. "What were you looking at before?"

Stephen navigated back to the webpage. "It's a site called MySpace. It's been around a little over a year. People can create profile pages."

Lizzie skimmed down the page on Stephen's computer. There was a picture of a young woman at the top and then a list of her favorite foods, books, movies, her birthday, and comments about what she was doing each day.

"It's networking on a whole new level. This is one of the girls on the list." Stephen pointed at the picture at the top of the screen.

"Why would she want to put personal information out there?" Lizzie studied the picture of a young woman with a heart-shaped face, brown eyes, and brown hair with streaks of bright red.

"I don't know. I heard about it from Jeffrey. He mentioned Michelle's band has a profile page."

Lizzie shifted her gaze from the website to Stephen. "I didn't know you and Jeffrey were friends."

Stephen shrugged. "When you and Ian were in Vermont, he needed someone to talk to and called me. We went out to dinner, talked about work and stuff. We've gotten together a few times since, usually when you and Ian were together and Michelle was busy. I seem to be his fall back call when everyone else is busy."

"Huh." Lizzie had a hard time picturing Stephen and Jeffrey hanging out. Jeffrey was a recovering alcoholic with a newfound faith in God. He was struggling to figure out who he was without the grief and anger he'd held onto for so many years. Stephen was a good kid, less than two years out of college. While he'd learned a lot from Lizzie in the past six months, he was still a bit awkward in social settings. Lizzie found herself wondering if Stephen believed in God, ashamed she'd been too caught up in her own problems to consider this before.

"She's the only one on the list with a profile here. There's nothing alarming on her page, but she does seem to go shopping an awful lot. I can't imagine the pay is that much better in Colorado, especially since she's only been with the resort five months."

Lizzie raised an eyebrow. "Her family could have money."

"Maybe. I'll see what I can find out. She works front desk, but can't be stealing from her cash bank since she's never been written up for missing money. Maybe she's getting big tips or maybe she's stealing credit cards."

"Surely the managers would have caught her if she was doing that."

"Depends on how often she did it. We'll see if her family has money before I start accusing her of stealing, though."

The door to the front desk opened and one of the cashiers stepped through carrying a vase filled with tulips in deep purple and bright pink hues. "Lizzie, these are for you," the cashier said as he placed them on the edge of Stephen's desk.

"Thank you." Lizzie reached for the card.

Dinner tonight, I'll pick you up at 6:30.
Love, Ian

"Are they from Ian?" Stephen asked.

Lizzie felt her muscles tense, then nodded, scooped up the vase and went back to her office.

CHAPTER ELEVEN

Sheila popped her head into the sun-filled office. "Mr. Cavanaugh?"

Ian looked up from his drafting table. "Sheila, how many times do I have to tell you to call me Ian?"

"You know I'm old-fashioned and still believe in speaking to my boss in a respectful manner." Sheila smiled. "Besides, if I called you Ian, I'd feel like I was treating you like my grandson."

"You aren't that old."

"No, I don't suppose I am. Here's the information on the restaurant." Sheila placed a neatly written piece of paper on the table. "They will hold a table no matter what time you arrive."

"Thank you for doing this. I owe you one."

"Have you talked to Lizzie yet?"

"She doesn't like me to call her at work so I sent her flowers and told her what time I'd pick her up."

Sheila pursed her lips.

"What? Isn't that romantic?"

Sheila rubbed her hands together. "For most women yes, but Lizzie might...well, she..."

"Might take it the wrong way," Ian finished for his diplomatic secretary. He ran a hand through his hair and groaned. "She's going to think I'm telling her what to do."

"That's a possibility."

"I should have learned by now that the grand gestures tend to backfire for me."

"Don't give up on grand gestures. One day she will appreciate them without reservations."

"I don't know, Sheila. If she doesn't know by now that I don't want to control her, that I don't want to use her, that all I want is to love her, what chance do we have?" Ian's heart ached at the idea of a future without Lizzie, but he didn't know how much longer he could overlook the walls she kept around her heart.

"You love her and you wait for her. God is working on her." Sheila placed an encouraging hand on Ian's shoulder.

"Should I call?"

"I don't know. If she's asked you not to, then that might make things worse. Maybe she'll call you."

Ian blew out a long breath. "I guess I'll just wait and see."

Sheila patted his shoulder then slipped out of the office. Ian stood and moved to the window. He watched the traffic streaming by, the sound of engines completely silenced by the thick glass. Even though he'd changed into fresh clothes, he still felt wrinkled, his heart in despair.

"Lord, I don't know what else to do to prove to Lizzie how much I love her. I thought we were in a good place when we left Vermont, but she is pushing me away again. Show me what she needs and how I can give it to her."

Ian leaned his head against the window. That's your problem, he thought. You're trying to give her what only God can. You can't heal her wounds or help her to love herself.

"Lord, let her know that I don't want to control her, that I only want to see her."

CHAPTER TWELVE

Dark clouds covered the sky, making the morning feel oppressive and cold. Jeffrey stuffed his hands in his coat pockets and kept his head down against the rising wind. He took the steps up to the office trailer two at a time. As he opened the door, a gust tugged at it, nearly slamming it back against the wall.

"Yikes," Jenny cried out.

"Sorry," Jeffrey mumbled. "It's going to be a nasty day."

"I put the plumbing bids on your desk."

"Thanks. I'll review them as soon as I get a cup of coffee."

Jenny smiled and held out a cup filled with a delicious-smelling brew. Jeffrey accepted it and took a sip. He didn't usually go for flavored coffees, but this was different. It was earthy and bold, without any bitter aftertaste. Something about it made him think of Lizzie. At the thought of her, Jeffrey's shoulder's sagged and he dropped his briefcase on the floor by his chair.

"Do you want me to try Gregory one more time?" Jenny asked.

"No, he's had his chance. Start the termination of contract paperwork. I'll let our guys know about the change." Jeffrey took another sip of his coffee. "Hopefully we can have the new contractor start Monday."

"Yes, sir. I'll have it ready for you to sign in an hour." Jenny sat down behind her desk and started typing.

Jeffrey let his mind drift. An image of Lizzie, up to her elbows in dirt as she planted a new garden, filled his mind. He knew Lizzie could never be more than a friend. The few weeks they'd tried dating had been awkward and he'd almost lost her completely. Still, he couldn't help wondering if there was something he could change, some way he could make it work between them.

Then there was Michelle. A picture of her on stage performing, her face glowing with excitement, replaced Lizzie in his mind. He'd felt drawn to her from their first meeting eight months before. He'd blown it then by being an obnoxious jerk. Now, when it seemed like he had a second chance, he was cautious.

He'd given his life to Christ, he'd gotten help with his drinking problem, and avoided friends he'd had during his wild days. He'd even started speaking to his parents again after being estranged for years. He wasn't sure if he could date Michelle now, unless she became a believer as well.

He knew how easy it would be for him to slip back into old habits. Going to the clubs on a regular basis to watch her play could open the door to drinking, which would lead him to do other things he would regret.

The trailer door blew open and wind filled the room, scattering papers in every direction. Jeffrey looked up to see Wally, one of the guys on his crew he'd become friends with. Wally tugged the door shut and dropped into a chair across from Jeffrey.

"I don't know how much work we can do in this weather," Wally said.

"There's plenty of electrical and plumbing that can be done on the lower floors. Hopefully the wind will die down enough to use the cranes this afternoon."

"Tim has a track meet this afternoon. I was hoping I could make it."

Jeffrey knew Wally's teenage son, Tim, had fallen in with a bad crowd and Wally had signed the kid up for track, hoping he'd find some more positive influences. So far, Tim hadn't seemed very interested in being part of the team.

"Is he actually going to show up for this one?"

Wally grimaced. "That's why I was hoping I could go, to make sure he does. Coach said if he misses this meet or any more practices then he's off the team."

"Maybe track isn't his thing. What about basketball or football?"

"He hates them both, said it's moronic to fight over a stupid ball." Wally shook his head." I don't know what else I can do."

Jeffrey thought the kid needed a healthy dose of reality. Wally had bent over backwards to give his son anything he wanted ever since his wife had died, but Tim kept pushing the limits. "Maybe it's time for some tough love," Jeffrey said.

"I've already taken away everything he loves. He hasn't been allowed to skateboard or hang out with his old friends for two months. He hasn't played video games in three months. There's nothing left to take away."

"I know I don't have any experience raising kids, and I know you've done your best for him, but maybe it's time to look for help."

"What kind of help?"

Jeffrey considered his next words carefully. "There's a group at my church for single parents."

Wally held up his hand. "Stop. I told you I don't believe any of that God stuff. I thought you were going through a phase or something, but I don't know what to think anymore. Have they brainwashed you?"

Jeffrey sighed and slumped back in his chair. "No, I haven't been brainwashed. How many times do I have to tell you?"

"You can't tell me you're happy with your life now. You don't ever do anything fun anymore."

"My definition of fun has changed, that's all. I'm not so sure I was even having fun before."

Wally laughed. "What's not fun about having beautiful chicks falling all over you, never having to worry about having a date? You were the golden boy."

Jeffrey winced at the memories, recognizing how many of those women he'd hurt with his callous attitude. "That's only fun when you don't know how to fill the void inside yourself any other way. I don't have to fill that void anymore."

Wally stood up and waved off Jeffrey's words. "So, you think I can leave early today?"

"If the wind hasn't died down by one, you can go."

Wally nodded and left the trailer, slamming the door behind him. Jeffrey reached for his coffee cup, but the drink had gone cold.

"I think it's nice you still try to help him," Jenny said.

Her quiet words reminded Jeffrey he wasn't alone. He cleared his throat. "I wish I could do more for him."

"He has to be open to hear what you are saying. Give it time."

Jeffrey remembered all the times Camylle had tried to talk to him about God, especially in her last days. It had taken him years to be willing to listen and open up when Lizzie shared her own faith with him. Jeffrey poured himself another cup of coffee and said a silent prayer for both Wally and Michelle.

CHAPTER THIRTEEN

Behind the closed door of her office, Lizzie read the card on the flowers again before crumpling it up and tossing it in the garbage. She considered dumping the flowers as well. Instead, she moved them from her desk to a filing cabinet where she wouldn't see them while she worked. She unlocked the computer screensaver and skimmed through her emails: a few simple inquires about upcoming guests and a list of requests from one of their frequent visitors. She hit the print key.

When she turned to retrieve the email from the printer, her eyes lingered on the tulips. They seemed to smile at her. Several of their half-opened blooms were tilting in her direction. She gnashed her teeth. Does he think he can command me to have dinner with him? She snatched the paper from the printer and spun her chair around, knocking her knee on the side of the desk. A yelp of pain escaped her lips before she could hold it back.

"Everything okay?" Stephen poked his head around the corner of the door.

"Yeah, I just hit my knee." Lizzie motioned for Stephen to come in. He approached her desk, his eyes studying her. "I'm fine," she insisted as she handed the list across the desk.

"Would you mind working on these reservations for Elaine Henderson? She's coming again in three weeks."

Stephen took the list and scanned it. "Most of her usual places. Shouldn't be a problem."

"Thanks."

Stephen turned to leave.

"Wait," Lizzie said as he reached the door. "Take the flowers and get rid of them."

"Aren't they from Ian?" Stephen returned to her desk.

Lizzie nodded but refused to meet his gaze. He sat down and leaned forward, placing his palms on the edge of her desk.

"What's wrong?" he asked.

Lizzie didn't know if she was going to cry or scream. Had it only been a few weeks since she and Ian had sat together in a Vermont ski-lodge and she'd told him she wanted a future with him? Ian was the best thing to happen to her in a long time, yet every time he knocked down one of her walls, she would push him away again.

"Did you have a fight?" Stephen pressed.

"No, he wants to take me to dinner tonight."

"And you don't want to go?" Stephen shook his head. "I'll never understand women."

Lizzie tried to laugh, but it came out as a croaking sob. Stephen was on his feet and around the desk, kneeling beside her and touching her shoulder.

"I didn't mean to upset you. It was a joke."

Lizzie swatted at the tears spilling from her eyes and reached for a tissue. "It's not you."

After blowing her nose, she sat up straight and looked Stephen in the eye. "I'm an idiot and don't deserve a man like Ian, but I'm so thankful he disagrees."

"Of course he disagrees. You two are perfect together." Stephen squeezed her shoulder and stood. "I'll take the flowers away if you really want me to, but I think you should keep them and you should call Ian. Tell him you can't wait to have dinner with him."

"Leave the flowers," Lizzie whispered.

"I'll make sure no one bothers you for a while," Stephen assured her as he moved toward the door.

CHAPTER FOURTEEN

Shadows danced on the drafting table as a stiff wind shook the budding branches of a sycamore tree outside the window. Ian's pencil moved swiftly across the page, his shopping center design taking a new direction. Trying to see the site through Lizzie's eyes had inspired him. Commercial projects tended to be banal. Sheila's words about parking taking precedence over landscaping had bothered him until he remembered a conversation he'd had with Lizzie during a Christmas shopping trip. After completing a section of the new sketch, Ian paused to study his work.

"Mr. Cavanaugh?" Sheila's voice came over the office intercom.

Ian slipped off his stool and crossed the room to pick up the phone. "Yes," he said, still thinking about the plan.

"I have Lizzie on the line for you."

Ian could hear the smile in his secretary's voice. "Put her through."

"Ian?"

"I'm sorry about the flowers, I didn't mean for it to seem like I was telling you what to do," Ian blurted out as soon as he heard her voice. "I wanted to call you but…"

"They're beautiful. I'd love to have dinner with you."

"Really?" He didn't hide his surprise.

"I didn't take it well at first, but I know I've been hard to reach lately. I'm sorry I sent the email so late last night."

"Will six thirty give you enough time to get ready? The reservation is at seven. I knew you might get home late."

"It's been quiet today. I should be able to leave on time."

"Great, I'll see you at six thirty then."

"Thank you, Ian. I love you."

"I love you too." He hung up and punched his fist in the air, as if he'd hit the game winning home run. Snatching his coffee cup by the handle, he bounded out of the office and found Sheila in the kitchen making a cup of tea.

"She didn't sound upset," Sheila said without looking up from her cup.

"I think she was, but thank God, something made her understand." Ian filled his own cup with hot water and chose a bag of blueberry and pomegranate from the variety of teas in a box on the counter. "Stephen must have said something. I'll have to thank him."

"So she agreed to dinner?" Sheila dunked her tea bag several times before removing it from the hot water and dropping it in the garbage.

"She did." Ian grinned, forgetting his earlier concerns.

CHAPTER FIFTEEN

"Heads up!" someone yelled as Jeffrey crossed the dirt lot between the trailer office and the work site.

Jeffrey looked up to see a crane with a beam swaying in a sudden gust of wind. He bit back the urge to shout obscenities at the crane operator. Instead he yanked a radio from its place on his belt. "What do you think you are doing? Get that beam on the ground."

"Yes, sir," the operator responded a few seconds later.

"And don't hit anyone with it." Jeffrey shook his head and continued toward the crane. By the time he reached it the operator was climbing out of the cab.

"I'm sorry, sir. The wind had died down and we thought it would be okay to move it into place."

Jeffrey nodded. "It's been a tough month, between the plumbers dragging their feet and all this wind. I don't want you guys taking any chances." Jeffrey looked at his watch. "Why don't you call it a day? I don't think the weather's going to improve in the next hour."

The crane operator nodded. "Thank you, sir. Maybe Monday will be better."

"I sure hope so." Jeffrey slapped the man on the back and moved on toward the rising building.

The first floor was quiet, so he moved on to the second. There he found plumbers working furiously in a dozen different rooms. They didn't stop to talk when he entered, but kept their attention focused on their work.

"It's a shame you weren't working like this the past three weeks," Jeffrey muttered. He climbed the stairs to the third and fourth floors, finding similar scenes. As the clock moved closer to five, he expected his phone to ring with a call from the plumbing contractor asking him to reconsider. He continued on to the eighth floor. The plumbers hadn't reached this level and exposed pipes protruded into what would one day be bathrooms and break rooms.

He leaned against a beam, the cold metal leaching heat from his body, and wondered how he could keep this project on schedule and budget if he kept encountering set backs. He'd seen delays before as a foreman, but the responsibility hadn't fallen on him. Now, he was the one in charge and would feel the wrath of his bosses if the client wasn't happy. The pressure weighed on him heavier today than it had since the last hurricane delay. His cell phone chirped and he noticed it was five minutes past five.

"Robbins," he answered.

"Jeffrey, how's it going? Sorry I wasn't able to get back to you sooner. I had to leave town on some personal business."

"Gregory, don't," Jeffrey tried to stop the man.

"Give us another chance. I have a new manager lined up for next week. He's my best guy. I took him off another project so we can get your job up to speed."

"It's too late. I already signed a new contract."

"Let me make this right."

Jeffrey hated the pleading tone coming from the other end of the line. "I'm sorry, Gregory. It's done."

Gregory sighed. "This isn't the way we usually work."

"We all have things that come up, I get that, but you need to make sure you have someone in the office taking care of business."

"I know. I didn't expect things to get this out of hand."

"Look, I'm not going to bad-mouth you, but I have to think about my business too."

"I appreciate that and I really am sorry."

"I hope whatever you have going on works out."

After Jeffrey disconnected the call, he descended to the first floor. Three of the plumbers were outside, loading equipment into their trucks. He got the impression they'd been waiting for him.

"Mr. Robbins." The youngest of the men stepped forward. "We wanted to apologize for the delays." The man pointed at himself and his friends. "We tried to get the other guys to quit goofing off."

"There are always a few who cause trouble for others. You may want to let your boss know who the troublemakers were, so they don't ruin any more jobs for you."

The young man nodded. "The first six floors are complete."

A burst of wind rushed around the corner of the building, lifting dirt in spirals around their feet. Jeffrey clutched at the hard hat still on his head.

"You guys better get home. Drive safe." Jeffrey waved and jogged to the trailer.

The door opened as he approached and Jenny stepped outside, her helmet of hair not moving in the wind. Jeffrey had to smile at the sight.

"If you don't need anything else, I'm heading out," she said, her eyes glancing up to the sky. Jeffrey looked up as well and found the clouds that had obscured the morning sky had darkened and seemed to be pressing down on them. Any minute they would let loose a torrent of chilling rain.

"Have a good weekend," Jeffrey said.

He ducked into the trailer just as the first large drops spattered the parched ground. He turned off his computer, locked up the cabinets, and looked in vain for an umbrella or raincoat. He cracked the door open, but couldn't see beyond the first step through the curtain of water. He shut the door and returned to his desk, dropping into the chair with a loud squeak.

He pulled out his cell phone and scrolled through his contacts. He hadn't called most of the numbers in months, not since he'd committed to living a life that would glorify God. When he got to Wally's number he considered calling. Tim's track meet was probably over by now, if it hadn't been rained out.

His finger hovered over the call button, then moved to scroll to the next name. If they got together, Wally would want to go out drinking. It may be raining downtown, but this was Florida and it may be clear as can be two miles away. Wally would find a bar unaffected by the weather.

Michelle's number scrolled into view and Jeffrey checked his watch. Already six o'clock. He tried to remember if she had a show this evening. He knew she was playing The Social on Saturday. Better not to bother her just in case.

Giving up, he stuffed the phone into his pocket and walked to the door. He cracked it open and found the rain had slackened to a heavy drizzle.

He stepped outside, keeping close to the building for the minimal protection it offered while he locked up. Then, car key ready, he dashed through puddles, mud covering his boots and splashing his pants. At the truck he fumbled with the key, slipping in and out of the lock. By the time he got the door open and climbed inside he was soaked through.

CHAPTER SIXTEEN

Stephen grabbed a frozen dinner from the freezer and popped it into the microwave, not bothering to check the heating instructions. When the microwave beeped, he took the plate of well-balanced yet bland food to the couch and kicked back, using his stomach as a table. A sitcom rerun played on the television, but Stephen's thoughts were on the girl in Colorado he'd been tasked with evaluating for Mr. Kingsley.

Kira Levenson, the subject of his investigation, had attended a community college for nine months before dropping out. She'd held a string of jobs in the service industry, never staying in one place for more than six months. The idea that she could be stealing from the resort without getting caught intrigued him. An exhaustive search into her background had found that she came from a lower-middle-class family scraping to meet their basic needs.

Sitting up, Stephen set his plate on the coffee table and reached for a file folder. He shuffled through the papers until he came to a photo of Kira he'd printed from her MySpace page. He studied the photo, staring into the eyes as if they would open the door to who this girl really was.

Kira's record at Snowcap Lodge was unremarkable. Hired in November of the previous year, she worked twenty to twenty-five hours a week, was always on time, and had only two call-ins. There weren't any disciplinary notes nor any commendations for outstanding work.

Setting aside the photo, Stephen opened up his laptop and logged on to MySpace. With a few taps of the keys he was on Kira's page and noticed she'd posted an update only ten minutes earlier.

Aren't these shoes just fab! Now I just need to score an invite to the McNally party next week. Anyone looking for a date?

Stephen studied the photo of Kira's feet clad in a pair of strappy sandals with three inch heels, trying to understand what made them "fab".

Another image appeared on the screen, the name brand now visible as she dangled the shoes from one finger.

"Jimmy Choo," Stephen mumbled, opening another browser window and typing in the name. He scrolled through the list of websites until he found a company page and clicked around that site until an image of the same shoes appeared.

"Are you kidding me? Six hundred dollars?" Stephen shook his head. At least when he spent sixty dollars on a pair of tennis shoes, he got a whole shoe, not a few straps and a sole. What were women thinking? He went back to Kira's page and took a screenshot to add to her file. "She certainly didn't buy those on her salary from the resort."

Stephen spent the next half hour surfing the Internet, searching for stories about Snowcap Lodge. Snowcap had an excellent reputation for service and community involvement. For the past six years the resort had given generously to a local children's hospital, Toys for Tots, and the American Cancer society.

An article on one small non-profit organization called Bear Necessities drew his attention. They worked to increase awareness of the presence of bears and how to avoid dangerous encounters while hiking or camping in the surrounding areas. There was a photo of volunteers participating in trail repairs at a nearby state park. Kira's smiling face caught Stephen's attention. The article didn't mention the names of any of the volunteers, but did have a quote from Snowcap's general manager.

"The opportunity to come together with other resorts and care for the environment is rewarding," said Rodney Peters, general manager of the Snowcap Lodge.

Stephen wondered which other resorts were involved in the effort and how well the employees might know each other. He considered sending the article to the general manager and asking for the names of the others in the photo. How do I interview anyone without Kira finding out I'm investigating her, he thought. Do the Ryland employees know Kingsley is vetting them, that they could lose their jobs in this merger?

He closed the computer, took his paper plate to the garbage, and opened the refrigerator. He stared at the sparse contents; a bottle of ketchup, some mustard, a tub of butter, a couple of sodas, some yogurt, and a wedge of cheese that was disappearing behind a layer of mold. He let the door fall closed and reached for his cell phone lying on the counter. After scrolling through his contacts he sighed and wandered back to the couch. Another Friday night, flipping through boring TV shows.

CHAPTER SEVENTEEN

Lizzie and Ian approached a shopping center that had seen better days. The paint was faded, weeds grew through cracks in the parking lot, and three of the five storefronts were vacant. Ian stepped out of the car and opened Lizzie's door.

"Where are you taking me?" Lizzie asked, grasping Ian's hand.

"It's a new place Sheila told me about."

"New? Looks more like it's about to go out of business."

"If it looks scary inside we can go someplace else."

"If we can get back out," Lizzie mumbled.

Ian opened the door and the scent of fresh bread and garlic wafted out to greet them. "Smells good," he said with a half smile.

A podium stood just inside the door, manned by a middle-aged woman with black hair pulled up in a loose bun, her cheeks colored with rouge that matched her lipstick. She reminded Lizzie of a gypsy she'd seen at a carnival when she was twelve.

"Good evening, you must be Mr. Ian and Ms. Elizabeth." The hostess smiled at them.

"Did Sheila send our photograph over?" Ian chuckled.

"No, but she did say you were a cute couple." The hostess winked. "Right this way."

The restaurant was long and narrow with twenty tables. The kitchen ran along the left side behind a wall of glass. The hostess took Lizzie and Ian to a table near the back of the restaurant and provided them with menus.

"The special tonight is rack of lamb with roasted garlic potatoes, but I also recommend the pasta primavera with squash and peppers. Your server will be Frederick and he will be with you in a moment."

When the hostess was out of earshot, Lizzie leaned across the table. "How does Sheila know about this place?"

"She said she knows the chef." Ian looked around at the empty tables. "Do you want to go somewhere else?"

"Don't go, it's still early." A man appeared at their table, a bottle of wine in one hand and two glasses in the other. "We don't usually get busy until around eight thirty. I'm Frederic and I have a bottle of pinot grigio for you, compliments of the chef." Frederick poured a small amount into a glass and waited for Ian to approve it.

"That's very good," Ian said.

"I'll give you a few minutes to look over the menu," Frederick said after he had filled their glasses.

"It can't be all bad if the chef already knows the wine I prefer." Lizzie took a sip then reached for the bottle Frederick had left chilling in a nearby ice bucket and studied the label. "Can you read the vineyard?"

Ian held the bottle toward the light spilling out of the kitchen, but shook his head. "We'll have to ask. I don't know how we are going to read the menus. Why does it have to be so dark in here?"

"It's romantic, love." Lizzie smiled and slid her hand across the table toward Ian's. He took it and lifted it to his lips.

CHAPTER EIGHTEEN

"You seem happy tonight. Good day at work?" Ian unfolded his napkin and placed it in his lap.

Lizzie shrugged. "Nothing special. Did I tell you Mr. Kingsley finalized the purchase of the Ryland properties?"

"Is that going to affect your job?"

"I don't think so, but Mr. Kingsley asked Stephen to review some of the Ryland employees."

"Wouldn't they have already gone through background checks when Ryland hired them?"

"Kingsley is having checks run again. He seems to think Stephen has a talent for spotting things that may not come up in a background check."

"Like what?"

Lizzie played with one of her earrings as she thought. "Stephen has a way of recognizing personality traits. That's one of the reasons I knew he'd make a good concierge. He has a natural ability to read people. He received a few names to look into yesterday and already has some questions about one girl in particular."

"What's her story?"

"I'm not sure. He showed me her profile page on MySpace; have you ever heard of that? Putting up pictures and personal information for anyone to see. Seems a bit crazy to me. Anyway, this girl shops...a lot."

"Isn't that what women do?"

Lizzie frowned. "Some more than others, but Stephen thinks she's buying high-end items that she couldn't afford on her salary."

"Maybe her family has money."

"He's looking into that. He didn't want to accuse her of her anything without finding out as much as possible."

Ian nodded. "He's a stand-up guy."

Frederick arrived with their entrées, a rack of lamb for Ian and pasta primavera for Lizzie. "Any fresh ground pepper or parmesan?"

"Yes, please," they both replied at the same time.

Frederick turned to Lizzie. "Ladies first."

"Parmesan." Lizzie watched as he shredded the cheese into a small pile on top of her pasta before gesturing for him to stop.

After grinding out a healthy sprinkling of pepper for Ian, Frederick stepped back from the table. "Is there anything else you need?"

Ian looked to Lizzie who shook her head. "Not at the moment."

"Bon appétit."

Lizzie mixed the cheese into her pasta and used her fork to cut it into manageable lengths.

"You know, if we ever go to Italy you'll have to learn how to twirl it on your fork. I think they would consider what you are doing sacrilegious."

"I guess you will have to give me some notice before the trip so I can practice."

Ian's hand dropped from the table to his pocket before he remembered it was empty. Instead he picked up his napkin and dabbed at his lips. "The lamb is incredible, do you want to try some?"

"Sure." She leaned forward and took a bite off his fork. The meat was tender and juicy, the flavors of rosemary, pepper, and thyme highlighting its sweetness. "Oh, wow."

Ian grinned. "Sheila's been holding out on me. If she has friends who can cook like this, who knows what other secrets she has."

"I hope she hasn't been keeping me a secret, I need all the publicity I can get." A tall man in a white chef's coat approached their table, his smile displaying perfect white teeth. "I'm Arnaldo and it's a pleasure to have you here tonight. I'm glad you made it in before the rush so I can say hello."

"Everything is delicious," Lizzie said.

"The best lamb I've ever had," Ian added.

Arnaldo's smile widened. "I'm happy if you're happy. What about the wine?"

"It's perfect. Where is it from? I couldn't read the label."

"It's from the Bressan Estate. I discovered the vineyard when I was training in the Collio region of Italy. When I opened this place, I knew it would have a prominent place on the menu."

"I've been trying to learn more about wine, but it's hard to keep straight the different things that can affect the taste," Lizzie admitted.

Arnaldo nodded. "You can only learn so much from books. You need to experience wine to understand it, to find what you enjoy."

"Have you considered offering wine seminars here?" Lizzie asked.

"I have, maybe one a month."

"Please let me know if you do. I think I'd enjoy that."

The chef rubbed his cheek and Lizzie could see the thoughts flashing behind his green eyes. "Weekend lunches have been slow. I will look into this more."

Lizzie restrained herself from clapping like an excited child. "How long have you been cooking?"

"Since I was a little boy. I used to drag a step stool up to the stove to help my grandmother cook."

The front door opened and a large party entered, their conversation filling the quiet restaurant. "That will be the Anderson party, twenty-fifth wedding anniversary. I must get back to the kitchen, but I hope to see you again soon."

Lizzie glanced to the window onto the kitchen and watched as cooks prepared their stations and sharpened knives. She could see Arnaldo calling out instructions, but the glass kept all of the kitchen noise at bay.

"I didn't know you'd been studying up on wine." Ian's word interrupted Lizzie's thoughts.

"I've been helping Tammy with the group menus lately. I thought it would be good to have a better understanding so I'm not always asking her or Chef Gustave what the best pairings are. Plus, the more I know, the more I can up-sell and the general manager is always looking for ways to increase revenue."

"Jeffrey's mother knows quite a bit about wine. I bet she'd be happy to help you."

"I suppose she does with all the functions her family attends." Lizzie cocked her head. "What about you? Do you know anything about wine? Your family is just as connected as the Robbins."

Ian gave a slight nod. "Yes, my parents are connected and they attend a lot of events in Connecticut."

"You have your own business, you have influential friends and clients. Why aren't you invited to the same functions as the Robbins?"

Ian raised his nearly empty wine glass and drained it. "Being invited and choosing to go are two different things."

Lizzie searched Ian's face for answers. Did she really know so little about him that she hadn't realized how important he was in this town? How could she ever fit into the world of exclusive parties and elite benefits?

"You don't have to fit into a world I'm not a part of," Ian said, reading her mind.

"How did you…"

"You were biting your lip."

"Do you ever miss it?"

"I left Connecticut when I was eighteen. I remember my parents getting dressed up for big parties. They always looked nice and they seemed happy when they left the house. A few times, I was awake when they came home and I could hear them complaining about the people." Ian closed his eyes and leaned back in his chair.

"One night mother was going on about how hideous one woman's dress was. How shocked she was that another had arrived with a man they all knew was the owner of a grocery store."

Lizzie tried to hear those words coming from the gentle, caring woman she'd met a few weeks ago. "I can't imagine your mother talking that way about anyone."

Ian chuckled. "Neither could I. When I heard father laughing, I crept out of my bed to the top of the stairs. He told her she did a fine impersonation of Mrs. Carmichael. They both laughed then. Mother said she didn't know how many more of these insufferable parties she could attend. I think that is probably when I decided I wouldn't be a part of it when I grew up."

"Couldn't those parties help your business, though?"

"Maybe, but I keep busy. I wouldn't want work handed to me because of my family." Leaning forward, he reached across the table and stroked her hand. "This way I have the choice of which doors to walk through and who I want by my side."

Lizzie's eyes met Ian's for a moment but she looked away as a familiar tension gripped her.

"Getting back to your original question, I know a little bit about wine. If Arnaldo decides to start offering seminars I could be talked into attending."

Lizzie looked toward the kitchen and caught Arnaldo looking in their direction. He winked before turning back to his work. "I hope he does. I think it would be fun."

CHAPTER NINETEEN

Sunlight peeked through the clouds as Jeffrey turned off Fairbanks Avenue. With the heater on full blast for the past ten minutes he'd finally stopped shivering and his short hair had stopped dripping. He pulled into his driveway and slid out of the truck, leaving a puddle of water in the seat. His socks squished as he approached the bungalow and pushed through the front door.

After a long hot shower, Jeffrey flipped on the television and scanned through the channels but nothing caught his interest. He pulled out his phone and within a few clicks it was ringing.

"Hello?" A surprised voice answered.

"Hey, it's Jeffrey. Are you busy?"

Stephen laughed. "Not exactly. What's up?"

"I gotta get out of the house. You want to go bowling?"

"Bowling? Really?"

"It's either that or go to a bar."

"Sure, bowling could be fun."

"I doubt that, but it's better than sitting home alone."

"True. Do you even know where there is a bowling alley?"

"Yeah, there is one on Aloma." Jeffrey gave Stephen the address and some basic directions and they agreed to meet there in twenty minutes.

A power ballad from the 1980s roared from speakers above the door as Stephen entered the bowling alley. The smell of nachos, pizza, and hot dogs made his stomach growl, the paltry frozen dinner forgotten. He scanned the faces of people milling around a pool table, then shifted his gaze to the bar area, and finally to the shoe rental counter. He caught sight of Jeffrey heading to a lane to the left of the rental counter. After getting a pair of shoes, Stephen made his way to the lane Jeffrey had claimed.

"You made it," Jeffrey said.

"Did you think I wouldn't?"

"I don't know. After we hung up I realized how lame this is."

Stephen looked around. People of all ages filled the lanes. "It must not be too lame since we aren't the only ones here."

Jeffrey chuckled. "True. I wouldn't have considered stepping foot into a bowling alley a year ago."

"I probably shouldn't tell you I almost went out on the pro-bowling tour then." Stephen sat down to change into the rented shoes.

"Seriously?" Jeffrey asked, his eyes growing wide.

Stephen tried to hold back his smile, but burst into laughter. "No way. I haven't been bowling since I was twelve. My mom sent me to an eight-week summer camp. I did get quite good, though."

Jeffrey stood and tested the balls in a rack behind the semi-circle of plastic chairs. Ten minutes later each had a ball they felt comfortable with.

"Why don't you keep score, since you are the master?"

Stephen nodded and set up the electronic scoreboard. Instead of using their names he entered Jedi Master and Young Padawan.

"Funny," Jeffrey said.

"Hey, I let you go first," Stephen retaliated in mock defense.

Jeffrey took several purposeful steps, his arm extended back, then swinging forward as he came to a stop just inches from the foul line. The ball flew two feet before dropping with a thud and curving into the gutter, bouncing from side to side to the end of the lane.

"That was just a warm up," Jeffrey said, stepping back to wait for his ball to return.

After a second gutter ball, Jeffrey sat down and Stephen took his place on the lane. Stephen allowed the ball to hang from his hand, swinging back and forth in a small arc, getting used to the feel of it. When he stepped forward, he glided, releasing the ball in a straight line, rolling faster and faster down the middle of the lane. With a loud clatter it hit the lead pin and the others went flying. Strike!

Jeffrey groaned. "It's going to be a long night, isn't it?"

Stephen strode back to his seat feeling better than he had in weeks. "I'm sure that was just luck."

"Uh-huh." Jeffrey grabbed his ball and flung it down the lane. It connected with two of the pins on the far right, leaving eight standing. His second attempt collected another three pins.

"You just needed to get your arm limbered up." Stephen slapped Jeffrey on the back as they passed each other.

Five frames later, Stephen's ball finally went into the gutter, and he ended the frame with three pins standing. "See, I'm not perfect."

"I should have gone to the bar," Jeffrey said, head down as he collected his ball.

Stephen stopped and reached for Jeffrey's shoulder. He turned the other man to face him. "I'm glad you called. I needed to get out."

"Why, so you could show me how much better you are than me?" Jeffrey glared at Stephen.

"I'm not trying to be better than you," Stephen insisted.

"Whatever." Jeffrey shook off Stephen's hand and turned back to the lane. He moved slower, knelt down as he released the ball and watched as it rolled toward the center pin, never wavering. When all the pins fell, he jumped and waved his hands above his head.

Stephen let out a small sigh of relief. "There you go, it just takes patience."

Jeffrey's smile faded and he took his seat without acknowledging Stephen.

They completed the game in silence, Stephen throwing more gutter balls, hoping to thaw the ice that had developed between them.

"I'm going to get some nachos," Stephen said. "You want anything?"

"I want a beer, but I'll take a bottle of water. You want to play another game?"

"Sure, if you want to. I'll pay for it on my way to the snack bar."

"Great. I'm going to hit the head." Jeffrey left before Stephen could respond, disappearing behind a crowd of rowdy teens at the rental counter.

Stephen ordered his nachos, a soda, and a bottle of water and stepped aside to wait for his order.

CHAPTER TWENTY

"Thank you for coming. Send Sheila my love." Arnaldo shook Ian's hand at the door to the restaurant.

"Let us know if you start the wine seminars," Lizzie reminded the chef.

"You will be the first to know, my dear." Arnaldo kissed her hand.

Outside, the air was chilly on Lizzie's bare arms. She shivered and Ian wrapped an arm around her. "I'm sorry I don't have a jacket."

"I'll be fine." Lizzie leaned her head on Ian's shoulder as they crossed the parking lot. Traffic on Sand Lake Road filled the air with exhaust and noise, but Lizzie inhaled the woodsy scent of Ian's skin. Tucked inside the car, the noise faded away. She leaned her head against the soft leather and closed her eyes.

"Do you have any plans this weekend?" Ian asked.

"Hmm?" Lizzie's eyes fluttered open and she found Ian gazing at her. "I don't think so. You?"

"The weather is supposed to be nice, maybe we could go to the beach."

Lizzie tried to remember the last time she'd been to the beach. "That sounds like fun."

Ian pulled out of the parking lot and joined the flow of traffic toward I-4. "Do you want me to pack a lunch or should we find a restaurant on the way over?"

"Let's take a picnic. I have a nice cooler from one of the groups that stayed at the hotel over the summer." Lizzie was growing excited at the prospect of spending the whole day with Ian. They hadn't had a chance to do so since returning from Vermont.

"I think I have a few beach towels," Ian said.

"I have beach chairs and sunscreen, should we bring a radio?" Lizzie started making a list in her head.

"Sure, it wouldn't be a day at the beach without some good music." Ian glanced at her and grinned.

By the time they pulled into her driveway, the trip was planned. Ian hurried around the car to open the door for her. They held hands as they walked to the front door. Lizzie had forgotten to leave the porch light on and the street lamp was too far away to provide illumination. Ian used a small pen light on his key chain to help her see the lock. When she unlocked the door, she pushed it open a crack, but didn't reach for the light switch.

"Thank you for dinner. I had a nice time."

"Me too." Ian reached up and cupped the back of her head with one strong hand.

Lizzie shivered, but not from the cold. She tilted her head up and met his lips. They were warm and soft and gentle. She stepped back, feeling the wood of the doorframe against her back. Ian moved forward and kissed her again. She squeezed his shoulder, pulling him closer, but he lifted his head and stepped away.

"Good night, my love." He traced his finger along the side of her nose, across her lips, then turned and made his way back to the car.

Lizzie was still slumped against the doorframe when his headlights came on and the car started down the driveway. She could barely breathe. She slipped around the edge of the door, locking it behind her and sinking to the floor. Maybe going to the beach wasn't a good idea after all.

CHAPTER TWENTY ONE

Stephen returned to the lane to find Jeffrey with a woman sitting on either side of him.

"Stephen," Jeffrey called in greeting. "I'd like you to meet Ashley and Fiona."

Stephen set the tray on a small table and exchanged pleasantries with the ladies.

"I met Fiona a couple of months ago," Jeffrey explained.

"I was surprised to see you in here," Fiona crooned, stroking Jeffrey's cheek with a slender finger.

Stephen thought he saw Jeffrey twitch uncomfortably at her touch, but couldn't understand why. She was gorgeous. Silky red hair trailed down her back and deep green eyes were enhanced by softly curving eyebrows. Her lips were full and seemed turned up in a perpetual smile. Her jeans and t-shirt were so tight they may have been painted on.

"I wanted to do something different," Jeffrey replied. "Would you like to join us?"

Jeffrey looked to Stephen who shrugged in agreement, unable to protest this invitation.

Fiona and Ashley exchanged a look before Fiona nodded. "Sure, we have time for one game."

"Great. Give me your shoe sizes and I'll add you to our lane." After the women provided their sizes, Jeffrey hurried to the rental counter, pushing ahead of a group of four older men who were next in line.

Stephen reset the scorecard and entered each of their names, conscious of the girls' eyes upon him.

"Which one of you was the Jedi Master?" Ashley asked.

He'd hoped they hadn't noticed the scorecard before he deleted it. "Um, that was a joke."

"Obviously," Fiona said, "but which one of you claimed that title?"

"You should probably chose a ball so we can get started when Jeffrey gets back."

Fiona laughed. "You can't use Jedi mind tricks on us, O great master."

Stephen felt his face flush and reached for his soda. Why did Jeffrey have to invite them to join us, he wondered.

"All set," Jeffrey said as he bounced back into the circle of chairs.

Ashley carried a pink ball with white swirls up to the line, squatted with her legs a few inches apart, cradled the ball in both hands and pushed it down the lane. Stephen watched it wobble so slowly he was sure it would stop before reaching either gutter or the end.

"Nice move, Ash," Fiona said. Stephen turned to find the pretty girl smirking at her friend.

"I told you I wasn't any good at this," Ashley said before scooping up a second ball.

"Hey, that's mine." Fiona jumped up from her seat, but Ashley had already sent it down the lane. This one moved faster and managed to knick one of the pins on the far right. Ashley turned, flipping her shoulder length brown hair as she did so.

Stephen watched the women, trying to figure out how they had ended up in a bowling alley on a Friday night. Ashley took a seat next to Jeffrey, tucking her legs up underneath her and leaning toward him.

Fiona waited by the ball return, tapping her fingers on the edge until the midnight blue ball she'd chosen appeared. Without a word, she stepped forward, sending the ball speeding down the lane for a perfect strike. Stephen heard Jeffrey groan and knew it wasn't in appreciation of Fiona's fine form.

"Show us what you've got, hot stuff," Fiona teased as she passed Stephen.

He could feel his palms grow sweaty and hoped he wouldn't drop his ball when he picked it up from the return tray. Taking several deep breaths, Stephen rolled his shoulders and crossed the wooden floor in three long strides, watching his ball spiral toward the pins, missing the head, but knocking down eight others.

"Not exactly what I'd call a master," Fiona called from her seat.

While waiting for his ball to return Stephen's competitive nature struggled with his desire to let Jeffrey win.

"Show her what you can do, Stephen," Jeffrey said as Stephen collected his ball again. Stephen met Jeffrey's gaze and saw a hard determination. Stephen straightened and sent the ball sailing, knocking the remaining pins down with a loud crash.

The rest of the game proceeded with the competition between Fiona and Stephen intensifying with each frame. Ashley continued to push the ball like an old lady, but Jeffrey's game steadily improved.

Stephen stepped up for his last turn, three points behind Fiona. He closed his eyes and blocked out the sounds of other bowlers. He focused on the lane and, in a fluid motion that had become natural, released the ball. Strike! Not wanting to wait, he picked up the ball Jeffrey had been using and threw again. Strike!

Before turning from the lane he could feel Fiona's glare burning into his back. He bit his lip to keep from smiling as he made his way to the ball return. He lifted his ball, turned his back on Jeffrey and the women without meeting any of their eyes, and proceeded to release the ball down the lane.

His stomach tightened as it began to curve to the left. The seconds ticked by, the ball seeming to slow until it nicked the head pin on the left side, nine pins went down, the last wobbled back and forth slowly, then faster, until it too fell.

Jeffrey gave Stephen a high-five as they passed each other, but Fiona only glared as Stephen took his seat at the scorekeeper's table.

Fiona stood, her rented shoes dangling from her fingers. "Ashley, why don't you return these for me?"

Ashley took the shoes without a word, grabbed her own and left. Stephen fiddled with the computer, his head titled so he could watch Jeffrey and Fiona out of the corner of his eye.

Fiona slipped an arm around Jeffrey's waist and pulled him close. "What do you say we get out of here, hit a club or two?"

"What about Ashley?" Jeffrey asked.

"I think she's worn out from all this excitement. Said she wanted to head home."

Jeffrey stepped away, sat down and started untying his shoes. "I don't know. Stephen and I were talking about grabbing something to eat."

This was news to Stephen, but he remained silent, getting up to collect his ball and return it to the storage rack.

Fiona sat down beside Jeffrey and leaned in close, whispering something Stephen couldn't hear. Stephen saw Jeffrey's fingers falter on the laces. Fiona reached down to help. Jeffrey looked up at Stephen.

Does he want to go with her or not, Stephen wondered. He couldn't interpret the look Jeffrey had given him.

Jeffrey shoved his feet into his sneakers, tucking the laces into the sides. He gathered up his rented shoes and stood abruptly. Fiona, who'd been leaning against him, nearly fell off her chair. "It's been fun, Fiona, but I'm really hungry. Maybe we'll catch up with you later." Jeffrey turned to Stephen. "Want me to return your shoes?"

Stephen hadn't taken them off yet, but he slipped out of them without even sitting down. Jeffrey picked them up and bolted for the rental counter, leaving Stephen and Fiona alone. Stephen looked around for Ashley, but she seemed to have vanished.

Fiona joined Stephen by the ball return, collecting the balls she and Ashley had used in the crook of each arm.

"Tell him you're tired and want to go home," she hissed.

"It won't matter," Stephen said. "If he doesn't want to go out, then he'll just go home too."

"I don't think so. He wants to go out with me, but feels bad about leaving you behind." She smiled and her face softened. "I could get Ashley to stay to entertain you if you'd like."

"She didn't seem to be in the mood for entertaining." Stephen took Jeffrey's ball to the rack with Fiona following behind.

"She's just upset I made her bowl. She'll be fine when we get downtown."

"You ready to go?" Jeffrey called from the edge of a table behind the seating area.

"Right behind you," Stephen said.

Fiona grabbed Stephen's hand. "Last chance. She will make it worth your while."

Stephen felt his heart pounding. "Maybe another time."

Fiona held on a second longer then let go. Stephen caught up with Jeffrey by the front door.

"Why aren't you going out with her?" Stephen asked.

Jeffrey looked back over his shoulder before responding. "She's too much for me tonight."

Stephen had no idea what that meant, but thought asking might reveal how uneducated he was when it came to women.

"I'm going to see *Tangled Web* at the Social tomorrow, you want to come along?" Jeffrey asked.

"Sure, what time?"

"They go on at ten. We could grab something to eat before; meet at Houlihan's around eight thirty?"

Stephen heard footsteps behind them and glanced back. Fiona and Ashley were gaining on them fast. "Heads up," Stephen whispered.

"Follow me out of here. There's a diner about two miles down the road. We'll stop there and hope they pass on by."

"See you in a few," Stephen said in a loud voice as he stopped at his car

CHAPTER TWENTY TWO

Jeffrey checked his rearview mirror as he turned into the diner's parking lot. Stephen's SUV followed right behind. The lot was crowded and Jeffrey had to circle around to the back of the building before finding a parking spot. Stephen passed and Jeffrey cut the ignition. Checking the mirror again, he saw a red sports car cruising to a stop behind him. The passenger window rolled down. Jeffrey couldn't see the driver, but his gut told him it was Fiona.

This chick doesn't give up, he thought. His cell phone vibrated on the seat next to him.

"Looks like she followed us," Jeffrey said.

"I noticed. What do you want to do?" Stephen asked.

"Maybe she doesn't see me."

"You're parked under a light, she sees you."

"Of course." Jeffrey drummed on the steering wheel with his free hand.

"Are you sure you don't want to go out with her? She seems nice enough and she's gorgeous."

"Last year she and I would have been back at my place an hour ago. Now, well if you weren't with me I'd be on the phone to Lizzie."

"She's out with Ian tonight," Stephen said.

Jeffrey ground his teeth, frustrated at Stephen's lack of help. The kid had to know his history; Lizzie had surely filled him in.

A car door slammed and Jeffrey looked into the side mirror. Fiona sashayed between his truck and a battered old Camaro next to him. When she knocked on the window Jeffrey didn't move.

"Are you going to answer her?" Stephen asked.

"I don't know."

Fiona knocked again. Jeffrey rolled down the window and turned to face her, the phone still held to his ear.

"Are you going inside?" Fiona asked.

"As soon as I finish this call."

"Mind if I join you?"

"I don't know. The whole reason Stephen and I were out tonight is because he's having some trouble and wanted to talk about it. We didn't get to do that at the bowling alley."

"Woman trouble? Maybe I can help."

"I don't have any woman trouble," Stephen whispered through the phone.

"No, I think he might be embarrassed to talk about it in front of you."

"I don't bite." Fiona fluttered her eyelids. "Unless you want me to."

Jeffrey's heart started racing again and he felt his resolve crumbling. "I'll call you back in a few minutes."

Jeffrey ended the call and dropped the phone into his lap. Fiona's hand reached through the window to Jeffrey's cheek. Her skin was cold and soft against his, yet it sent a jolt of electricity through to the core of his being. He leaned forward and met her lips. They tasted like cherries and he hungered for more. The door handle pressed into his thigh, then his phone vibrated again. He pulled back, scrambling for the phone. When he met Fiona's gaze, her eyes glittered with a look of triumph.

"Hello?" Jeffrey tried to steady the quavering in his voice.

"I'm going to head home," Stephen said. "You have fun."

"No, I'll be right there."

"You don't have to."

"Really, I do."

"Go, help your friend. I'm sure I'll see you around." Fiona slithered back to her car, squealing the tires as she pulled away.

"I'll meet you inside." Jeffrey rolled up the window and ran a hand through his hair, massaging the top of his scalp for a long minute. His mind screamed, God, where are you? What are you doing to me?

When he stepped out of the truck, his legs felt weak. He used the edge of the vehicle as a crutch until he stopped shaking, then jogged around to the front of the restaurant.

Seated in a corner booth, with menus blocking their faces, Stephen cleared his throat. "It looked like Fiona was changing your mind about eating."

Jeffrey lowered his menu. Stephen peeked over the top of his own.

"How much has Lizzie told you about my past?"

"Your past? Nothing, just how she met you, all you did to help renovate her house. You introduced her to Ian too, didn't you?"

"Yeah, I did," Jeffrey said, swallowing the bitterness that grated against his mind at this reminder. "But she really didn't tell you about the problems I had when we met?"

Stephen shook his head. "She doesn't gossip about people."

Jeffrey slumped back and closed his eyes. "She really is the best person on the planet."

Jeffrey opened his eyes and leaned forward, resting his elbows on the table. "I'm an alcoholic and I've made several truckloads of bad decisions. Lizzie showed me the way out of that life, she helped me to accept Christ into my life."

Jeffrey paused and rubbed his eyes. "That doesn't mean I'm not tempted every day to return to my old life. In many ways it was a lot easier. I met Fiona at a bar a couple months ago, during one of my moments of weakness."

"You seemed happy to see her," Stephen said.

"More like surprised. A bowling alley doesn't seem like her scene. It's been a rough week. The kind of week I would have drowned in a bottle of Jack Daniels, so when I saw her I reverted back to my old self. I knew she was interested in me that night in the bar and she still seemed interested tonight. It was a boost to my ego," Jeffrey smiled. "As you said, she's beautiful."

"It's a bit creepy that she followed you here, though, isn't it?"

Jeffrey shrugged. "She had a goal and didn't give up."

CHAPTER TWENTY THREE

A light rain spattered the windshield, turning the streetlights into starbursts. Jeffrey didn't turn the wipers on until the windshield was completely covered with the tiny drops. The dry blades stuttered across the glass, leaving streaks that were more disruptive to his vision than the rain had been.

A traffic light twenty yards ahead turned yellow. Jeffrey eased his foot off the gas, preparing to stop. Headlights flashed in his rearview mirror. The car behind was running too fast to stop. Jeffrey accelerated, passing through the intersection as the light turned red.

He heard the screech of tires from behind, seconds before he felt the impact. His truck surged forward, slipping on the wet road. The steering wheel jerked to the right, spinning the truck ninety degrees. He could see headlights moving toward him, his body stiffening in anticipation.

There was a horn blast, squealing rubber, then the crunch of metal. He heard a loud crack and his arms, which gripped the steering wheel, went limp. His head whipped forward and jerked back.

The blare of a siren cut through the air, and flashing red and blue lights reflected off the dark windows of closed shops. Jeffrey felt something running down his cheek and tried to reach up to wipe it away, but his arm wouldn't move. The seatbelt pulled tight across his chest and left shoulder. He struggled to reach across his body to find the release button.

"Sir, don't move," a confident voice called. "An ambulance will be here soon."

Jeffrey turned to look out the window. Sharp pain radiated down his neck and across his shoulders.

"Be still until the paramedics arrive," the voice repeated. "I'm going to check on the other drivers."

Jeffrey closed his eyes, grinding his teeth against the intensifying pain. He heard another siren in the distance, and then everything grew quiet.

The groan of twisted metal being moved roused Jeffrey. He didn't know how much time had passed, but he could see an ambulance through the spider web of glass that used to be his windshield. He felt something hard being wrapped around his neck and tried to struggle.

"It's okay, we're trying to stabilize your neck before we move you," a man said.

It took several seconds for the words to sink in, and then Jeffrey relaxed. When the collar was secure, the man stepped back and Jeffrey noticed he wore an EMT uniform.

"Can you feel your feet?" the man asked.

Jeffrey wiggled his toes, all ten at once. "Yes," he said.

"Good. I'm going to see if I can unlock your seatbelt." The man leaned across Jeffrey and pushed the release button several times.

There were so many flashing lights now that Jeffrey felt sick. He closed his eyes, but the lights didn't go away.

"Stay awake, buddy. I'll have you out of here in a snap." The man pulled a knife from his pocket and used the seatbelt cutter in its handle to tear through the material. Jeffrey felt an instant release of tension. The man unthreaded the belt from the restraining lock, tucking it under the seat.

"Now we're going to put you on a spine board."

Jeffrey saw two firefighters approaching with a long board. They placed one end of it on a stretcher, and then he felt them slide the other end under his left thigh.

The first EMT gripped Jeffrey's shoulders. "I'm going to rotate you so your back is on the board. We're going to take this slow."

When he was clear of the truck, they slid the board onto the stretcher and secured it using a series of belts.

"Any pain here?" the EMT asked as he felt along the bone of Jeffrey's leg.

"No, I think my legs are fine, but I'm pretty sure my arm is broken."

The EMT moved to the arm. "The wrist is broken and it looks like your collarbone may be too. You have a nasty gash on your head. Do you know if you lost consciousness?"

"Maybe for a few minutes. I don't remember you guys arriving."

The EMT nodded then pulled a small flashlight from his shirt pocket. He clicked it on and shined it in Jeffrey's eyes. "Follow the light, please."

The light seemed extraordinarily bright and Jeffrey squinted against it, trying to track it's movement.

"Most likely you have a concussion. When we get you loaded into the rig, I'll clean up your cuts. Is there anyone we can call for you?"

"My phone, it was on the passenger seat."

"I'll have the police check for it. Anyone in particular we should look for?"

Jeffrey thought about telling the paramedic to call his mother, she should know, even if they were still on tentative terms. "Speed dial number two."

"All right. Give us a minute then we'll get you to the hospital."

Jeffrey closed his eyes again.

CHAPTER TWENTY FOUR

Lizzie turned back the covers on her bed and sat down. She reached for a tube of lotion and rubbed some on her hands, the scent of lavender and vanilla soothing her racing mind. Her evening with Ian had been lovely, making her forget why she wanted to put distance between them, until that kiss goodnight. The thought of it made her breathing grow shallow. She lifted her scented hands to her face and made herself inhale deeply.

How much longer can I hold on without crossing the line, she wondered. I long to be with him. She took another deep breath, the lavender and vanilla clearing her mind.

"Get a grip," she commanded herself. "This is a good relationship. Ian isn't going to push you to do anything and you aren't going to tempt him."

Sure you are. She heard the words as clearly as if they'd been spoken by someone else in the room. *Once you've tasted passion you can't resist it.*

"Yes, I can," she whispered.

No you can't. Deep down you want it more than you even know.

"Maybe I can't resist it on my own, but I can through Christ Jesus who strengthens me." Lizzie rose from her bed, her declaration growing louder with each word.

That old crutch? When are you going to toss that aside and think for yourself?

Lizzie dropped to her knees, her head resting on the edge of the bed. "Lord, where are you? Rescue me from these thoughts, strengthen my heart against these temptations."

Lizzie waited for a comforting voice to reassure her, but there was none. Minutes passed, her hands gripping the bedspread tighter and tighter. No encouragement came, but no more whispers of fear or temptation came either. She released the bedspread and wiped at the tears now trailing down her face.

Her cell phone vibrated on the bedside table followed by the chorus of the Randy Newman song "You've Got a Friend in Me".

"Jeffrey, it's late. Can we talk tomorrow?"

"Miss, this is David Evans with the Orlando Police Department."

"Police? What's wrong?" Lizzie raced across the bedroom to the dresser. She opened two drawers and yanked out a shirt and jeans before the man could reply.

"Mr. Robbins has been in a car accident. We're taking him to Florida Hospital, Orlando."

"Have his parents been notified?"

"No, ma'am. He asked us to contact you."

"Is he going to be all right?"

"He's pretty banged up, but nothing life threatening."

"Thank you, officer. I will contact his parents."

Lizzie hung up and dressed quickly. As she slipped on a pair of sandals, she scrolled through her contacts until she found the number for Mr. and Mrs. Robbins.

CHAPTER TWENTY FIVE

Bright lights illuminated the hospital parking lot. Lizzie navigated her car into the first parking spot she could find, then raced into the emergency room lobby. Jeffrey's parents couldn't have made it here before her, but she scanned the faces in the waiting room, checking just the same. She made her way to the front desk where a young mother stood, holding a crying baby. Lizzie patted her leg impatiently while the mother listed the baby's symptoms to a bored-looking clerk.

"Lizzie!" a voice called. She turned to see Jacquelyn Robbins rushing through the sliding glass doors. "Where's Jeffrey?"

"I just got here," Lizzie said. "Where's Edward?"

"He's parking the car. What do I have to do to get news of my son?"

"Can I help you?" the bored clerk asked.

Lizzie wrapped an arm around Jacquelyn's shoulders and guided her to the desk.

"My son was brought in, he was in a car accident. I need to see him." Jacquelyn's voice trembled.

"What's his name?"

"Jeffrey Robbins."

The clerk entered the name into a computer, but didn't speak for what felt like hours. Lizzie wanted to reach across the counter and shake the man.

"Looks like he's still being evaluated. I'll put a note in that you're here and someone will come to get you when you can see him."

"What? Why can't I see him now? Is he okay?" Jacquelyn gripped the counter with both hands.

"Let the doctors do their job, ma'am. They'll let you know as soon as you can see him."

Lizzie gave Jacquelyn's shoulders a reassuring squeeze and half dragged, half guided her to a brown plastic chair. Lizzie glanced back to the door and saw Edward Robbins entering, his face red and breathing heavily. She waved to him.

"Where's Jeffrey?" he asked as he dropped into a chair beside his wife.

"They won't tell me anything or let me see him," Jacquelyn said.

Lizzie wanted to comfort them, but she was scared and frustrated too. She closed her eyes and said a silent prayer for peace and guidance.

"Did you call Ian?" Jacquelyn asked.

Lizzie opened her eyes and shook her head. She hadn't even thought of calling Ian.

"I'm so happy he and Jeffrey are friends again. Ian is such a nice young man." Jacquelyn reached for Lizzie's hand.

A door opened and a man in green scrubs stepped into the waiting room. "Mrs. Robbins?"

Jacquelyn stood. "Here I am."

Jacquelyn and Edward followed the man through the doors, leaving Lizzie alone. She retrieved her cell phone from her purse and pushed the speed dial for Ian.

"Miss me already?" His teasing tone was warm and comforting.

"Jeffrey was in a wreck. I'm at the hospital waiting to find out more."

"Which hospital?"

She could hear the jangle of his keys and the slamming of a door. "Florida Hospital on Rollins Street."

"I'll be there as soon as I can."

"You don't have to."

"I'm on my way."

Lizzie hung up and bent forward, elbows on her knees, head in her hands. Was it only an hour ago that Ian had dropped her off after their dinner? With Edward and Jacquelyn gone, Lizzie became aware of the others in the waiting room. She could hear the crying baby and the mother humming a soft melody. A couple of teens whispered together then filled the room with raucous laughter. Several people were coughing and clearing their throats of phlegm. Underneath it all was a television, playing some reality show that no one was watching.

Unable to sit still any longer, Lizzie pushed out of the uncomfortable chair and paced around the room, hands shoved in her pockets. She made three circuits of the room before she sensed a change.

Ian strode toward her, crossing the distance before she took a single step. He pulled her into his arms and held her tight. Lizzie leaned into his chest, absorbing his warmth and strength.

"What happened?" he asked.

"I don't know. A policeman called me from Jeffrey's phone, said he had been in an accident and I was the person he wanted notified. I called his parents on my way here. They went back to see him a few minutes ago."

Lizzie allowed Ian to lead her to a pair of chairs. When they were seated, he brushed her cheek with his thumb.

"I'm sure he's going to be fine," Ian said.

Lizzie leaned her head on his shoulder and reached for his hand. They passed the next half hour in silence, the other patients being taken back one-by-one. By the time Jacquelyn returned, a whole new set of patients were waiting to be seen. Lizzie and Ian rose in unison and met Jacquelyn in the middle of the room.

"He has some broken bones and a concussion, but no internal injuries," Jacquelyn said, her relief evident.

"Thank the Lord," Lizzie replied.

"He asked if you were here," Jacquelyn said, her gaze directed at Lizzie. "He wants to see you. Would you mind waiting a little longer? He's being admitted overnight for observation."

"Sure, we can wait," Lizzie said. "Is there anything I can do for you or Edward?"

Jacquelyn shook her head. "Thank you, dear. I'll call you as soon as we get to the room and give you the number."

Lizzie and Ian returned to their seats after Jacquelyn left. "Why do you think he had the police call you instead of his parents?" Ian asked.

"I don't know. Maybe he worried it would be too upsetting for them."

"He had to know you would call them, though."

Lizzie shrugged. "Their relationship is better, but there's a lot of heartache and distrust for him to put behind him."

Lizzie's cell phone rang. She answered and stood up. "Room 412, got it. We're on our way."

CHAPTER TWENTY SIX

"Hey guys." Jeffrey smiled when Lizzie and Ian stepped into the room. "Will you please tell my parents to go home and get some rest?"

Lizzie glanced at Jacquelyn and Edward sitting in chairs at the end of the bed. "They just want to make sure you're all right."

"I'm beaten up, but I'll live."

"What happened?" Ian asked.

"Some guy was tailgating me. I was coming up on an intersection and the light was yellow. I couldn't stop or he would have been on top of me. I sped up but he kept coming and hit me from the rear sending me into a spin. I guess there weren't any cars waiting at the stoplight for the other direction, because then someone blew through and crashed into me. Not sure what happened to the tailgater. He had to have been hit too."

"What about your truck?" Lizzie asked.

"No idea where it is right now. I'll have to contact the police tomorrow."

"I can do that for you," Edward offered.

Jeffrey turned to his father. "You don't have to."

"I want to. The doctor told you to rest."

Jeffrey hesitated and closed his eyes for several seconds. "Okay, if you want to, that's fine."

"Is there anything Ian and I can do for you?" Lizzie asked.

"Would you call Michelle and let her know I won't be able to make it to her show tomorrow night? Her number is in my phone." Jeffrey frowned. "Oh, and call Stephen too. He was going to go with me."

Jacquelyn extended the cell phone to Lizzie.

"Anything else?"

"Rain check on lunch tomorrow?" Jeffrey smiled.

"Oh yeah," Lizzie blushed. "I had forgotten about that." Lizzie entered Michelle's number into her own phone, then placed Jeffrey's on the nightstand.

"You need me to call anyone at your office?" Ian asked.

"No, I'm hoping to be sent home tomorrow."

"We should go so you can get some sleep." Ian turned to Edward and Jacquelyn. "Give me a call if you need any help getting him home."

Jacquelyn nodded.

Outside the hospital, the rain had stopped, leaving a damp chill in the air. Ian twined his fingers with Lizzie's as they crossed the parking lot to her car.

"You were supposed to have lunch with Jeffrey tomorrow?" he asked.

Lizzie looked at the ground. "It slipped my mind. He texted me last night."

"Maybe we should skip the beach."

Lizzie lifted her head. He met her gaze and saw relief flicker in her eyes. Ian's stomach tightened with fear, or was it anger?

"But I want to spend time with you," she whispered.

He leaned forward and kissed her forehead. "It's been a long day. We'll talk tomorrow."

"Ian," Lizzie said.

He stepped back, letting go of her hand. "Good night, Lizzie."

Lizzie opened her door and slipped inside. He waited to hear the door lock, then turned away and weaved through the lot to his own car. He slammed the door harder than he intended and started the sporty engine.

"Why, O God, why can she make plans with Jeffrey, but I have to beg for her to see me?" His words rang like the cry of a spoiled child in his ears, but he no longer cared.

The kitchen light was still on when he returned to his condo. A small box on the counter caught his eye and he charged across the room. He scooped up the box and squeezed it, as if trying to get juice from it, then threw it. It hit a pillow on the couch with a loud thwack and bounced onto the floor. The walls of the condo seemed to push in on him. He turned his back on the taunting box and retreated through the front door.

CHAPTER TWENTY SEVEN

Saturday mornings were Michelle's favorite time. She could cuddle up in bed as long as she wanted and dawdle over a pot of coffee once she did manage to get up. This morning was overcast and the sun didn't break through the slit in her curtains until after nine. She checked the clock with one groggy eye before rolling over, turning her back to the invading sunlight. She had just found a comfortable position and was drifting off again when her phone rang.

Her answering machine picked up, but the caller didn't leave a message. Michelle growled at whoever had disturbed her and pulled her blanket tighter. The phone rang again, and she kicked back the covers, rolled across the bed and snatched up the phone.

"What?" she barked into the receiver.

"Michelle?"

"Yeah, who is this?"

"Lizzie Reynolds, I'm a friend of Jeffrey's."

Michelle hesitated. Jeffrey had been trying to introduce her to Lizzie for weeks, but she'd never dreamed he'd give out her phone number without her permission. "Look, it's too early for a discussion on religion."

"That's not why I'm calling," Lizzie said. "It's about Jeffery. He was in an accident last night. He wanted me to let you know he won't be able to make your show tonight."

Michelle sat up. "What happened? Is he okay?"

"He's got a broken collar bone, a broken wrist, and a concussion. He stayed in the hospital overnight, but should be released today."

"If he's okay why didn't he call?" Michelle felt panic choking her.

"I don't know." Lizzie hesitated, realizing it was strange he'd asked her to call. "Maybe he wasn't thinking clearly, because of the concussion."

"You're sure he's all right?"

"He looked okay last night, and I'm sure the doctor wouldn't be planning to discharge him today if there were any concerns." Lizzie paused. "Are you okay?"

Michelle ran a hand through her tangled hair. "Yeah, surprised I guess."

Lizzie laughed. "Jeffrey can do that."

Michelle sighed. "Yes, he can. Thanks for letting me know. Do you think he will be up for company today?"

"You can always call. I don't know when he might be released from the hospital."

"Right."

Lizzie didn't speak for several seconds and Michelle thought she may have hung up.

"Michelle, you can call me any time. You have my number now."

"Yeah, okay." Lizzie's casual offer unnerved Michelle. In her life, strangers didn't offer compassion, much less friendship.

They ended the call and Michelle got out of bed. There was no way she was going back to sleep now. She padded into the kitchen and started a pot of coffee, then turned on the television to a 24-hour news station. The reports of murders, house fires, and a mudslide in California were depressing. She turned the television off and poured herself a cup of coffee and a bowl of cereal.

The coffee, hot and strong, helped bring her scattered thoughts into focus. By the time she'd finished her cereal she had a plan.

The hospital parking lot was busy with people coming and going. From her back seat, Michelle pulled out a basket and waited for a car to pass before crossing to the hospital lobby.

The door to Jeffrey's room was closed. Michelle knocked softly with no response so she knocked again, harder.

"Come in."

Michelle pushed the wide door open, wondering if this had been a good idea after all.

"Hey." Jeffrey smiled and pushed himself up on his pillows.

"I brought you some comfort food," Michelle said, lifting the basket in front of her.

"Thanks." Jeffrey's gaze dropped to the basket and Michelle set it on the bed next to him. He pulled out a bag of Doritos and grinned. "I love these. How did you know?"

"I didn't, but they're one of my favorites when I'm not feeling well. Since I don't know where you live, I thought I'd catch you here. No one should have to recover without some treats."

"You want to sit down?" Jeffrey gestured toward a chair at the end of the bed.

"I don't want to tire you out."

"Don't worry about me. I feel fine."

"Fine, really?" Michelle raised her eyebrows. "You look like you lost a fight with a bull."

"I could use the company to distract me from the pain. They don't even have basic cable here."

"Have you heard when you will be released?"

"The doctor came by almost two hours ago, but I'm still waiting on some paperwork to be completed."

"Do you have someone coming to pick you up?"

"My parents told me to call when I get the release order."

"I can drive you home, if you'd like."

"I don't want to be a bother. You have your show tonight."

"That's hours from now and it wouldn't be a bother. I want to help."

"It may be a while yet before I am sprung."

"Mr. Robbins?" a nurse asked as she stepped into the room.

"Yes," Jeffrey said.

"I have your discharge paperwork."

Michelle giggled. "Your timing couldn't have been better."

"I guess I will take you up on your offer," Jeffrey said.

"Are you ready to go, then?" the nurse asked.

"Yes, ma'am."

The nurse handed him several papers and showed him where to sign. "I'll have a volunteer bring a wheelchair up."

"I don't need it," Jeffrey protested.

"It's hospital policy," the nurse replied then smiled. "And it keeps our volunteers busy."

A few minutes later, a bright-faced teenage girl pushed a wheelchair into the room. "I hear we have someone ready to go home."

Jeffrey transferred into the wheelchair. "Ready to roll."

Michelle followed behind the young volunteer, fishing in her purse for keys. When the elevator reached the ground floor, Michelle stepped out first.

"I'll run out and pull the car up to the door," she said.

"We'll meet you there," the volunteer replied.

Michelle jogged out to her car and grabbed the papers cluttering the passenger seat, tossing them into the back. When she pulled up to the front door, Jeffrey and the volunteer were waiting. The volunteer pushed the wheelchair closer and Jeffrey settled himself into the car.

Michelle pulled into the driveway of Jeffrey's bungalow and cut the engine. "Cute place."

"It's not much, but it's home." Jeffrey tried to remember how messy the living room had been when he'd left to go bowling. He pushed open the car door and stood. His whole body ached like he'd hiked twenty miles uphill then rolled all the way back down.

Michelle moved to his side and offered her arm, but he waved her away. He pulled his keys from his pocket and leaned against the door as he fumbled with the lock.

"I apologize in advance for the mess," he said as the door swung open.

Michelle followed him inside, carrying the goody basket. Jeffrey scanned the room, relieved to find only a couple of magazines and a soda can on the coffee table. He made his way to the couch and sat down with a sigh.

"Where would you like me to put this?" Michelle asked, holding up the basket.

"The coffee table is fine."

"Is there anything I can get for you? Do you need something to drink?" Michelle looked toward the kitchen.

Jeffrey knew the sink was full of dishes and doubted there was much in the refrigerator. "No, I'm fine for now. I should call and let my parents know I'm home."

"Of course." Michelle stepped toward the door.

"Sorry I'm going to miss your show tonight," Jeffrey said.

"I think you have an acceptable excuse this time," Michelle teased.

"Thanks again for the snacks." Jeffrey didn't want her to leave yet, but didn't want to seem needy either.

"You can call if you get bored. We don't go on until ten." Michelle adjusted her purse on her shoulder.

Jeffrey nodded. "I know you guys will be great."

Michelle waved and stepped outside, the door closing softly behind her. Jeffrey fished his cell phone out of his pocket. After he let his mother know he was home and assured her he didn't need anything, he stretched out on the couch and fell asleep.

CHAPTER TWENTY EIGHT

A ringing sound woke Ian from a deep sleep. He rolled over and tumbled off the narrow couch. The fall startled him awake. He found his phone on a nearby table and reached for it. The caller ID displayed Lizzie's name, but he didn't answer. He wasn't ready to talk to her yet.

More awake now, he stood and stretched. Dusty light fell through the office window onto the papers on his drafting table. He moved through the outer office, past Sheila's desk and entered the small kitchen. He heated water and chose two bags of English Breakfast tea, dunking them into the water until it turned almost as dark as coffee.

He took his cup back to his office and straddled the stool at the drafting table. Behind him, his phone rang again, but he ignored it. He studied the top sketch. It was a drawing with peaks and arches that gave it an old world feel, but had a wraparound porch that was pure southern charm.

There were three other house designs as well, but he was continually drawn back to this first sketch. He picked up a pencil and made some adjustments to the design and added in some landscaping. He stepped back to view it from a distance and nodded, satisfied it was complete.

His cell phone rang and he reached for it without thinking. "Hello?"

"Ian, are you all right? I've been calling and calling."

He turned away from the drafting table and dropped onto the couch. Lizzie sounded frantic. "I've been working. I must not have heard the phone."

"I've been so worried."

"You're too busy to talk to me for days, now I don't answer the phone a few times and you're worried?" Ian's jawed tightened as he spoke. His stomach growled and a dull ache started at his temples.

"I...work has...I thought..." Lizzie stammered, not completing a single thought.

Ian could hear the strain in her voice. "Look, I'm hungry and tired. I don't think we should talk right now. I'll call you later."

"Ian?" Lizzie whispered.

Ian hesitated a second, then clicked the end button and turned the phone off. He looked back at the house plan, and with a raging swipe, sent all the papers flying around the office.

CHAPTER TWENTY NINE

An alert pinged on Stephen's computer and he clicked to find a new email message. He recognized the address of his friend Jason. He'd met Jason the first day of college and they'd hit it off right away. Both communications majors, they'd shared numerous classes and worked together on the student newspaper. Jason had moved to Colorado the previous year and Stephen seemed to remember he worked for a hotel out there. Unable to sleep after the bowling fiasco, he'd turned his attention to the investigations for Mr. Kingsley, and sent off an email asking Jason if he knew anything about the Snowcap Lodge.

Hey, Stephen.

Great to hear from you. I worked part-time at Snowcap Lodge before I got my job at Stratosphere Communications. It's a nice resort and everyone I met seemed to like working there. It's a busy place during ski season, but stays steady all year. They get a lot of convention business in the spring and summer. I'm still friends with several people there. What kind of information are you looking for? Give me a call and I'll see how I can help.

Jason

Stephen checked the clock before reaching for the phone. It was almost ten in Colorado. He dialed Jason's number and waited.

"Hello?"

"Jason, it's Stephen. Thanks for replying to my email."

"Steve-o, great to hear from you. How are things in Florida? You still working for that hotel?"

"Yeah, I'm still at Hotel Lago. It's not as bad as I thought it would be."

"I was sure you were going to be handling the cover-ups for the next Exxon spill or airline crash. How did you get into the hotel business?"

Stephen felt his face flush with embarrassment. He'd been sure he'd land a job in public relations after college. Three internships with major corporations, six months of freelance work at the tail end of his last internship and no job. When he'd been told his contract was up and there wasn't going to be a renewal due to some corporate restructuring, he'd been at a loss. Another three months had passed before he'd gotten the job at Hotel Lago as a last resort, to keep bill collectors at bay.

"It's not like you hit the ground running, either. You said you worked at Snowcap."

Jason laughed. "You got me there. It was only temporary, though."

"Did you happen to work with a girl named Kira Levenson?"

"Kira? The name sounds familiar. I'd probably recognize her if I saw her. You have any photos?"

Stephen flipped over to his web browser and pulled up her MySpace page. "I can email one right now. Are you at your computer?"

"Give me a second." Stephen could hear Jason moving. "Firing up my email now."

"The file should be there any second." Stephen gripped the phone tighter.

"Yeah, I remember her. She's cute. She had only been with the company a couple of weeks when I left. You planning some kind of long distance romance?"

"Not exactly." Stephen wondered how much he should tell Jason. "Can I trust you to keep a secret?"

"Sure, it's not like we know many of the same people anymore. What's going on?"

Stephen proceeded to tell Jason about the task Mr. Kingsley had given him and his own concerns regarding Kira's spending habits. "I don't want to get her into trouble if she can legitimately afford all these things."

Jason let out a long whistle. "You're a regular Sherlock. I'm impressed."

"Don't be. I've worried myself into an ulcer since Mr. Kingsley asked me to do this."

"I understand your concern about getting this right. If she's buying shoes as expensive as you think, she'd had to save every penny she made for an entire month."

"That's what I was afraid of." Stephen looked at the photo of Kira and his heart sank.

"It just so happens, I'm going to the McNally benefit she mentioned on her post. My boss is tight with Roger McNally and purchased several tables. Want me to see what I can find out?"

"She can't know I'm investigating her," Stephen said.

"No worries. I'll have her eating out of my hand and telling me all of her secrets by the end of the night."

"How are you going to manage that?"

"Leave it to me. I'll call you when I have more information."

"Are you sure you want to do this?" The excitement in Jason's words worried Stephen.

"Are you kidding? This is going to be fun."

"All right, but keep it quiet."

"Sure thing. Is there anyone else at the resort you are looking into?"

"There are four others, but I doubt you would know any of them. They all started after Kira so you would have been gone already."

"Give me their names and I'll see what I can find out."

Stephen retrieved the list of names and read them off.

"Any particular reason they are under the microscope?"

"The only thing I can guess is that they are the newest to the resort. Nothing notable on their records at Snowcap or any of their previous employers, according to the background check."

"I'll see what I can find out. Like I said, I still have some friends working there."

Stephen remembered the Bear Necessities volunteer photo. "One more thing. Would you mind if I sent you another photo to see if you recognize anyone?"

"Do they work at Snowcap as well?"

"I'm not sure, it's from a volunteer event that several resorts participated in."

"No problem, I'll give it a look."

"Thanks, Jason. I owe you one."

"I'll call you soon."

When Stephen hung up, he checked Kira's profile page once more and couldn't help smiling when he saw the new post.

Hello, gorgeous. I have tickets to McNally, where can I pick you up? The screen name the offer came from was LJ. Jason had been dubbed "Loquacious Jason" several years before. Those who knew the whole story shortened it to LJ.

Kira replied within minutes. *You're my prince. Meet me at the food court in Skyview Mall.*

The plan was already in motion

CHAPTER THIRTY

Wind ruffled Ian's hair as he raced down the highway, windows down and sunroof open. He squinted against the sun, which was sinking below his sun visor. The engine purred in delight as he shifted gears. After downing a double cheeseburger, fries, and large soda at a fast food joint near his office, he'd hopped in the car with no destination in mind. He wanted to get as far from Orlando as he could. He needed distance between himself and Lizzie and Jeffrey.

Signs for the junction of the 408 expressway with the Florida Turnpike flashed past and he downshifted to make the tight curve. He didn't need to slow for the toll, the express pass in the windshield beeping as he passed under the electronic bridge. Half an hour later, civilization dropped away as he passed marshland, interspersed with lakes and orange groves. The only change he noticed when the turnpike merged with Interstate-75 was the increase in traffic. Nearing Gainesville and the University of Florida he slowed, taking an exit that promised three gas stations, four restaurants and two hotels.

He coasted into a gas station and stepped out of his car. He thought about calling Lizzie, but shook off the urge. He hadn't been a priority to her for weeks. With the car fueled up he had to decide where to go next.

A Holiday Inn sign next to the gas station was inviting and his back ached. He drove across the shared parking lot and found a spot near the lobby entrance. Minutes later he closed the door to his room and sank onto the bed.

The room was quiet and smelled of roses. He lay back on the bed and closed his eyes. It felt good to stretch out. His night on the couch had given him cramps in his neck and lower back. He retrieved his phone from his pocket and turned it on for the first time in hours. There were seven missed calls, six from Lizzie and one from his mom.

He dialed and waited. "Hi, mom," he said when she answered.

"Hi, honey. How are you?"

"Not so great. How are you?"

"What's wrong, sweetie?"

"I don't think Lizzie's the girl for me. I think I have to end it."

"Are you sure? The two of you seem so happy together."

"I feel like a yo-yo, mom. She let's me get close then pushes me away again, but doesn't seem to have any problem getting close to Jeffrey." Speaking his former friend's name left a bitter taste in his mouth.

"She is complicated, I'll give you that, but love is about not giving up during the tough times."

"I just don't know if I have the energy any more. I feel like I have to beg her to spend time with me, but if Jeffrey sends her a text she's there in a flash. That speaks volumes to me."

"Do you really think there is an attraction between the two of them? From my conversations with her, I got the impression they were just friends with a lot of common baggage."

"Baggage I can't compete with. If she wants to keep living in the past then she can, but I want to start building a future."

"Have you talked to her about this?"

"Not since Vermont. She promised me then she was going to let go of the past so we could move forward."

"Maybe you need to talk to her again. Give her a chance to explain what she's feeling."

"What's to explain? She obviously doesn't want to spend her life with me."

"Ian, I know how much you love her. You were both happy during the ski trip. I also know how hard it was for her to understand our love and acceptance of her. She's scared underneath the confidence she's cultivated. Tell her how you are feeling. Go see her now."

"I can't."

"Why not? Is she working?"

"No."

"Then what's stopping you?"

"I'm not in Orlando."

"Where are you?"

"Gainesville. I had to get away. I got in the car and just started driving."

"Oh, sweetie. I wish I could give you a hug."

"Thanks, mom. Maybe I could come home for a few days, clear my head. I finished the plans for my current project yesterday. Sheila can send them to the client."

"Your father and I would love to have you visit, but you aren't one to run away from your problems. Straighten things out with Lizzie, then if you still want to come home the door is open."

Ian sighed. "You're right, of course. Does dad know how lucky he is to have you?"

Cassandra chuckled. "You can always remind him the next time you talk."

"Love you, mom."

"I love you, too. Call me soon."

"I will." Ian hung up and dialed into his voicemail. Lizzie had only left one message. Her voice was hoarse and he knew she'd been crying.

"Ian, I'm so sorry. Please don't hate me, please talk to me."

He didn't delete the message, but instead of calling her back he started texting.

I need some time to think. I'll call you tomorrow. I love you.

Before she could respond to his message he turned the phone off again.

CHAPTER THIRTY ONE

The buzz of her cell phone on the coffee table alerted Lizzie of a new text message. She lifted her head from the couch cushion then dissolved into fresh tears after reading Ian's words. Her life seemed to be crumbling around her.

A few hours earlier she'd received another message from Jacob Phillips advising her that his plans had changed. He would be in Florida with his wife the following Friday and hoped it would be okay to stop by that night. She hadn't responded to his message yet, afraid his visit meant they were thinking of either claiming the house for themselves or putting it on the market to sell. Either way she would be left homeless after putting so much of herself into the renovation.

Her gaze dropped to the hardwood floor that Ian had repaired not once but twice, after a hurricane had left the house flooded. Those floors had brought the most wonderful man into her life and she'd managed to drive him away.

Her phone rang with Jeffrey's ring tone. "Hey," she answered half-heartedly.

"What's wrong? You sound worse than I feel."

"It's been a bad day. Are you home?"

"Yeah, and boredom is about to drive me crazy. What do you do when you can't drink, play poker, or use one of your arms?"

"Watch a movie? Eat a pint of ice cream? Sleep?"

"I've already watched two movies on Lifetime. Are women really as dumb as they're portrayed in those movies?"

Lizzie couldn't help laughing. "My college roommate and I used to love spending Saturday on the couch, watching Lifetime movies. We said it was great training in what not to do when there is an intruder in your house. Why don't I bring over some ice cream and a couple of real movies?"

"You sure? I don't want to interrupt anything."

Lizzie snorted. "The only thing you're interrupting is my own pity party. I'll be there in half an hour."

She selected a couple of DVDs from her collection, stopped at a nearby convenience store and arrived on Jeffrey's doorstep twenty minutes later.

"That was fast," Jeffrey said when he opened the door.

"I brought *Braveheart, Die Hard*, and *Raiders of the Lost Ark*."

"What kind of ice cream goes with that much blood?"

"Red velvet, of course."

Jeffrey laughed. "I hope you brought some Rocky Road too."

"Would I forget your favorite ice cream?" Lizzie pulled two pints from the shopping bag and dropped the DVDs on the coffee table. "What do you want to start with?"

"You going to tell me what's got you so upset?"

"Not until I've eaten at least half of this ice cream."

She could feel Jeffrey's eyes following her as she moved into the kitchen for a pair of spoons and a couple sodas.

"All right, I guess we should start with *Raiders*. I can't remember the last time I watched it."

Jeffrey settled back on the couch and accepted the spoon and soda Lizzie offered him.

"Thanks for understanding," she said as she took her place on the opposite end of the couch.

"This is good," Jeffrey said, dipping his spoon into the ice cream container.

Lizzie pointed the remote control at the television and started the movie. "Harrison Ford and ice cream make everything better."

They finished their ice cream fifteen minutes into the movie and left the empty cartons on the coffee table. Lizzie curled into a ball, resting her head on the edge of the couch, letting herself get lost in the movie. She and Jeffrey laughed at all the same spots and slowly her tension eased. Spending time with Jeffrey had always been easy and comfortable.

When the movie ended, Jeffrey replaced it with *Die Hard*, taking the ice cream cartons to the garbage while the opening credits ran.

"Can I get you anything while I'm up?" he called from the kitchen.

"No, thanks," Lizzie said without lifting her head.

She watched Jeffrey wash his hands in the sink before opening the refrigerator for another can of soda. He plopped down on the couch and propped his feet on the coffee table, shooting a smile in her direction.

"I hope Ian doesn't mind me stealing you away for a few hours."

Lizzie closed her eyes against the tears that threatened. Why did he have to mention Ian? She felt Jeffrey's hand on her bare feet and opened her eyes, but didn't meet his gaze.

"What's wrong?"

"I really don't want to talk about it," Lizzie murmured. "Can't we just watch the movie?"

She knew Jeffrey was studying her, looking for answers she wasn't willing to offer. His hand remained on her foot a minute longer, then with a tender pat he let go.

Lizzie tried to focus on the movie, but the warmth of Jeffrey's hand lingered in her memory. He understood her better than anyone else. He knew when to push and when to let her work things out on her own. Why couldn't Ian do the same? Why did he make her feel so awful for trying to protect herself?

"Why didn't you and I try harder to make a relationship work?" she whispered.

Jeffrey paused the movie and dropped his feet off the table. "What did you say?"

"You heard me or you wouldn't have stopped the movie." Lizzie sat up and turned to face him.

"Where is this coming from? What happened between you and Ian?"

"This is about me and you," Lizzie insisted.

"No, it's not." Jeffrey ran his uninjured hand through his hair and released a long sigh. "This is about you and your fear of getting too close to him."

"You and I are close, I'm not afraid of that," Lizzie protested.

Jeffrey shook his head. "It's different and you know it. I love you dearly and I will always be thankful for the ways you changed my life, but we don't have chemistry."

"Just because a few kisses were awkward doesn't mean we don't have chemistry."

Jeffrey slid across the couch, closing the distance between them in a heartbeat, his lips upon hers before she could move away. The kiss was soft and warm, she wanted to give into it, but her heart wasn't racing and her body felt like stone.

"Nothing, right?" Jeffrey asked when he pulled away.

"You caught me by surprise, that's all."

"Has Ian never caught you by surprise? Have you felt as cold in his arms?"

"Stop it," Lizzie croaked, the tears now falling without reserve.

"You feel safe with me because you never feel out of control. We are both afraid of falling back into past patterns. When we are together we don't have to put on any masks about who we are, we can relax knowing there's no judgment. I don't know about you, but that gives me the strength to put the mask back on when I go out into the real world."

Jeffrey tilted Lizzie's chin up so she had to look him in the eye. "You don't have to be afraid of Ian. He is the most honorable man I've ever known. He and I may never be good friends again, but you have a real shot at a life with him. Don't blow it because you are scared."

"He deserves better than me."

Jeffrey shook his head. "There isn't anyone better than you, Lizzie."

She leaned in and rested her head on his chest. "He's not even speaking to me right now."

"He will. He's crazy about you, but you have to stop pushing him away. He's a good guy, but even his ego can only take so much. He will break at some point. Then he will stop trying to get you to let him in."

CHAPTER THIRTY TWO

As comfortable as the bed was, Ian found himself awake, staring at the ceiling when the sun started peeking through the curtains. He'd requested a wake-up call for seven, and didn't feel any pressing need to get up before then. He could hear the shower running in the room next door and wondered who the occupants were. Did they have big plans for the day? Were they in town to visit the college, or were they on business? He hadn't noticed much about the surroundings the previous night and wasn't even sure how far he was from the University of Florida.

The phone rang and he flopped a hand over to pick it up. A recorded message wished him a good morning and advised this was his wake-up call. He swung his feet over the edge of the bed and rubbed his face with his hands.

In the bathroom, his reflection showed two days of stubble. His eyes were bloodshot with purple circles underneath, and his dark hair was matted to his skull. He turned on the cold water, letting the sink fill, then dunked his head. The shock was bracing. When he lifted his head, streams of water dripped onto his shirt and the bathroom counter. He reached for a towel and patted his face dry, then ruffled the towel over his hair before dropping it on the counter. He used his fingers to comb through his hair and shape it into something less vagabond looking.

Next to the television he found a small coffee pot and a bag of coffee. "Come on, come on," he grumbled, waiting for the machine to brew.

He couldn't find cream or sugar so he downed the bitter liquid, relishing the caffeine jolt. He collected the express checkout bill from under the door, made sure there were no unexpected fees, and shoved it into his pocket. The smell of fuel and exhaust fumes assailed him as he stepped outside. A dozen cars lined the pumps at the gas station next door and a steady stream of traffic passed on the road.

He started up his car and gave the engine a minute to warm up while he checked the glove compartment for a cell phone charger. "If this was Lizzie's car, there would be two chargers. She always seems prepared for anything."

Not finding a charger, he tossed the cell phone into the passenger seat without turning it on. Any calls would have to wait until he returned home. Putting the car into gear, he backed out and joined the flow of traffic, taking the curve onto the interstate as fast as he dared.

CHAPTER THIRTY THREE

Lizzie stretched and opened one eye, the smell of fresh coffee teasing at her nose. When she saw Jeffrey standing over her, she jerked awake.

"How did you sleep?" Jeffrey asked as he handed her a cup of coffee.

"Pretty good. This is a comfortable couch."

"Yeah, I've passed out on it a number of times, but never during a battle scene. I think you made it through the first twenty minutes of *Braveheart* before you went off to dreamland.*"*

"I'm sorry." Lizzie took a sip of the coffee.

"That's okay, I was getting tired myself. You didn't get cold did you? I only had the one extra blanket." Jeffrey motioned to the blanket Lizzie now had wrapped around her shoulders.

"No, I was fine." She took another sip of the coffee then stood. "I should get home, though."

"Are you going to talk to Ian?"

Lizzie handed the coffee cup back to Jeffrey. "I don't know what to say, but I know I need to. Hopefully he will take my call."

"Go home and pray. God will give you the right words." Jeffrey pulled her into a hug.

"Who would have thought those words would come out of your mouth a year ago?" Lizzie giggled.

"Let me know how it goes." Jeffrey walked her to the door and waited for her to get into her car.

Lizzie turned the radio in her car off and made the drive in silence, praying for guidance, courage, and wisdom. By the time she reached her house, she felt more confident about the talk she needed to have with Ian. Her cell phone was dead so she went to her room and put it on the charging station while she took a hot shower.

Twenty minutes later she emerged in a pair of sweat pants and a cozy t-shirt and checked her phone, but there were no missed calls or text messages. She punched the speed dial for Ian and waited. It went straight to voicemail.

"Ian, it's me. I'm sorry for everything. Please call me." She glanced at the clock and wondered if he might be at the early church service. If she dressed quickly, she might be able to catch him as he left. She donned the first dress she found and a pair of shoes, ran a brush through her hair and raced out the door.

CHAPTER THIRTY FOUR

It was ten minutes past ten when Ian took the exit off the 408 expressway onto Interstate-4. The first worship service ended at ten, but Lizzie often went to the second service which didn't start until ten forty-five. Maybe he could catch her there. The interstate had light traffic, but the church parking lot was a bustle of activity: people still leaving from the first service or from early small group classes as well as those just arriving.

Ian's eyes searched each face for Lizzie. When a parking spot opened in front of him, he darted the small car into it and jumped out of the driver's seat, not even bothering to lock the doors. He hurried through the crowds, ignoring several greetings called out from acquaintances. He had eyes only for Lizzie.

Inside the foyer, which stretched the entire length of the church, the crowds thinned as people started taking their seats. He stepped inside the sanctuary and scanned the backs of heads, looking for her blond curls, but there were hundreds of people milling around.

The praise band took the stage and started playing "Who am I" by *Casting Crowns*. Ian slumped against the wall.

"Would you like to sit with us, sir?" A young woman holding a toddler touched Ian's arm, inviting him to join the pew where two other youngsters were seated beside her.

"Sure, thanks." Ian pushed off the wall and slipped into the row. He heard one of the children snicker as he passed by, and realized he must look awful, wearing the same clothes for the past two days.

He forced himself to stop scanning the congregation and focus on the worship songs. He didn't sing along but listened to the words, as if hearing them for the first time. Each song seemed to speak to where he was in his life this very minute. He closed his eyes and listened, opening his heart to the whispers of the Holy Spirit.

The pastor took the platform and opened with announcements and a word of prayer. "Open to Psalm 27, and please stand to honor the reading of God's word."

Ian reached for the copy of the Bible available in every pew and stood as he flipped through the pages to the right Psalm. He followed along as the pastor read.

"The Lord is my light and my salvation, whom shall I fear? The Lord is the stronghold of my life, of whom shall I be afraid?"

The words swam before Ian's eyes, his vision blurring through burning tears.

"For in the day of trouble he will keep me safe in his dwelling, he will hide me in the shelter of his tabernacle and set me high upon a rock."

Ian thought of all the promises he'd read in the Bible, how many verses he'd memorized that offered strength and encouragement, yet he hadn't recalled a single one during the past weeks as he struggled with the hurdles Lizzie seemed determined to place between them. He'd been trying to overcome the obstacles on his own.

"I am still confident of this: I will see the goodness of the Lord in the land of the living. Wait for the Lord; be strong and take heart and wait for the Lord."

Ian slipped the Bible back into the pew rack and dropped into his seat, head in his hands, trying to control the sobs that threatened to burst out of his broken heart.

"It's unclear if David wrote this song before he became king of Israel or closer to the end of his life, but he starts off with a lively faith, triumphing in the light and strength God offers. How often do we sing praise like this in our daily lives?" The pastor paused, giving the congregation a moment to reflect. Ian didn't need the pause, his heart had already reflected and found him lacking.

A tiny hand reached out and took hold of Ian's. Through his tears he could see the little girl next to him, looking at him with concern. Her fingers gripped his tightly.

"It's okay, mister. God loves you too," the little girl whispered.

Ian pulled a handkerchief from his pocket and dabbed at his face, then nodded at the little girl. "I know He does. I'm just sorry I haven't loved Him back enough lately."

The little girl's face remained serious. "That's okay too. He will forgive you if you ask Him to."

"You are a smart little girl. I hope you always remember how important it is for you to wait on God to work in your life. There will be times when you want to do things on your own, but only in God's timing can things work out the way He has planned."

"It's hard to wait sometimes. Like at Christmas, it's hard to wait to unwrap my presents. Sometimes I try to peek at them."

Ian suppressed a laugh. "There are things that are even harder to wait for when you get older. I'm glad I was reminded of that today."

The little girl held his hand for the rest of the service and Ian was grateful for her tender heart.

CHAPTER THIRTY FIVE

When Lizzie didn't find Ian among the crowd leaving after the first service, she considered going home, giving into her depression and crawling into bed. Then a friend of Ron and Emma's invited Lizzie to join her for the next service. Lizzie struggled to remember the woman's name.

"I hear Ron and Emma are on another trip to Africa," the woman said as they took their seats.

"Yes, they left a couple of weeks ago and will be gone until August. I received a letter from Emma a few days ago, letting me know they arrived and are excited about this adventure."

"The trip I went on with them last year changed my life, but I don't know if I could do it full-time like they do."

"It's certainly a calling, but they love it." Talking about her friends made Lizzie miss them more than ever. If Emma were here now, they could talk about the trouble with Ian. Emma had become a surrogate mother to Lizzie and the two shared everything.

"Next time you write to them, will you say hello for me? I'm terrible at keeping up with correspondence."

Lizzie smiled and nodded, wishing she'd gone home after all.

When the pastor asked the congregation to turn to Psalm 27 and stand for the reading of scripture, Lizzie obeyed, holding her Bible in front of her, opened to the passage but not looking at it. Her gaze drifted around the massive room, searching for Ian's face. Maybe he had gone to one of the small group classes earlier and that was why his phone was off. Maybe he was in this very room right now. From her position on the front left side of the church, she could see about a quarter of the congregation. Ian was nowhere to be found.

"Though an army besiege me, my heart will not fear; though war break out against me, even then will I be confident." The pastor paused. "Are you confident today? In this verse David shows us that he is confident he will be safe from the threat of outside armies; that God will protect him and even set him above fear of an attack."

Lizzie's gaze stopped roaming and zeroed in on the pastor. How was David so confident in God's provision? Wasn't he the guy who had to fight off invaders more than once and even his own son ended up trying to kill him? This Psalm must have been written before all that, she thought.

My child, why do you question my provision after all I have given you? The words whispered through her soul as clearly as if the woman next to her had said them. Lizzie shook her head and tried to focus on the pastor again.

Was giving my son not enough forgiveness for you? Do you need more from me?

Lizzie looked to her left, but the seat next to her was empty. She turned to the right, to the lady. Alice was her name, Alice Engelbert, it all came back in a flash. Alice gave Lizzie a questioning look.

"Are you okay?" Alice whispered.

Lizzie nodded and Alice returned her attention to the sermon. Lizzie closed her eyes and leaned back in the pew. I'm listening, Lord, she thought. The words of the pastor were the only thing she heard, but they were more of a drone than anything else. She kept her eyes closed, and from time to time a word or phrase would pierce her haze; shelter, rock, sacrifice, be merciful, wait for the Lord.

I am waiting, she thought. How long do I have to wait? The service was winding down and the band was returning to the stage for the invitation music.

"If you are struggling and need strength to wait on the Lord, I want to pray for you," the pastor said. "Let's all bow our heads and close our eyes. If you need strength, slip your hand up and let me know. Thank you. In the back, thank you. You aren't alone. There are times when each of us needs strength and prayer support from others. Don't be afraid to ask for that help."

Lizzie hesitated, then lifted her hand.

"On the right, thank you. Lord, I lift up to you all those who raised their hands. You know their circumstances and you know what they need. I pray that you will provide them with the strength and courage to face the armies standing against them. Lord, thank you for providing us a way to come before you, through your son, Jesus Christ. Thank you for His sacrifice that washes us clean from all sin when we accept your gift of salvation.

"There are several members of the church staff at the front here. If you would like to come forward and have one of them pray with you, please feel free to do so while we will sing 'Just as I Am'."

Lizzie stepped out of the pew and made her way to the front of the church where a woman in a dark blue dress met her. They knelt together and Lizzie let the woman place a hand on her back, washing her in prayer.

CHAPTER THIRTY SIX

Ian didn't need a hymnal to sing the chorus. He'd known this one since he was a small boy and the words came without a thought. Movement at the front of the church caught his attention. He directed his gaze toward the woman leaving her pew and making her way to the platform.

He looked down at the little girl, who still held his hand. "I need to go up front."

"I can pray for you here," she offered.

"Thank you, but I really need to go to the front."

She poked her lip out and squeezed his hand tighter.

"I know your prayer would be special, but there is someone up there I have to see."

"Are you sure?" She looked up at him with eyes that melted his heart.

"If it wasn't really important, I wouldn't go."

The little girl thought a minute, then nodded and let go of his hand. Ian excused himself past three other people at the end of the pew and hurried toward the front of the church. He worried that Lizzie would slip away before he made it to her.

When he passed the first pew, he noticed a man coming toward him, and recognized him as the pastor for the young adult ministry. The pastor extended a hand in greeting and steered Ian toward a section of steps not occupied by others who had come forward for prayer.

"Um, I didn't exactly come up for prayer," Ian whispered.

"There's no need to be embarrassed. No one is judging you," the young pastor replied.

"Really, I'm good. For the first time in weeks actually." Ian turned his head so he could see the others kneeling to his left. Lizzie was still there, but the woman she was with was standing up.

"Thank you, pastor, but you will have to excuse me." Ian sidestepped him, and in five long strides, was behind Lizzie. He knelt beside her and put an arm around her shoulder. Her head came up, nearly crashing into Ian's nose. When she recognized him, she fell into his arms, clinging to him.

"I'm so sorry," she whispered, her breath hot against his cheek. "I've been so afraid of temptation, of pushing us to go too far. I didn't mean to completely push you away, just far enough so I wouldn't have to be afraid."

Ian laughed and stood, drawing her to her feet, then lifted her off the ground. "Is that all? Then why don't we just get married?"

"What?"

Ian lowered her so her feet touched the ground again. "It's not the way I had planned it, but every time I've tried to ask, something happened."

"When have you tried to ask?"

"I had planned to on our sleigh ride in Vermont, but when we got stranded out there, I didn't think it was the best time. Then when we were playing Monopoly, but Jeffrey called. Since the trip there have been half a dozen times, but something always interfered. None of that matters now." Ian got down on one knee and took her hand.

"Elizabeth Christina Reynolds, will you marry me?"

"Yes, yes, yes." Lizzie wiped at the tears running down her face. Cheers and applause erupted from the congregation.

"Well, I can't say I've had that kind of reaction to a sermon before," the pastor quipped. "I can't wait to get the whole story. Why don't we close in prayer?"

Ian and Lizzie stood together, the pastoral staff on each side. Pastor Donovan stood behind them and placed a hand on each of their shoulders. "Lord, you work in miraculous ways. Only you know what truly happened here this morning, but I pray for your blessings upon these young people. Help them to keep you at the center of their lives together. As we go out into the mission field today, help us to share the light of your love."

CHAPTER THIRTY SEVEN

Sunlight bathed the church campus, warming the cool breeze as Lizzie and Ian stepped outside. Lizzie clung to Ian's arm; afraid she was going to wake from this dream.

"Where did you park?" Ian asked.

Lizzie blinked, looked around, and laughed. "I don't remember. I was so anxious to find you."

"Why don't we take my car, get some lunch and I can bring you back later?"

"Okay."

A line of cars waiting to exit the parking lot started honking, the occupants waving as Lizzie and Ian passed.

"We made quite a spectacle, didn't we?" Ian said.

Lizzie didn't answer, but waved back to the well-wishers. When they reached Ian's car, he pulled her close and caressed her face. Lizzie felt her stomach flutter. She leaned into his tender kiss, joy pulsing through her body.

"Harvest Cafe?" Ian asked as he held the car door open for her.

Lizzie nodded. Located a few blocks from the church, the cafe was small enough to go unnoticed by the masses leaving the large church campus. Lizzie and Ian had discovered it by accident several months earlier and it had become a favorite retreat. Ian navigated through the dense traffic to a quiet side street.

There were only two other cars in the parking lot of the cafe. Ian pulled into a spot close to the front door and hopped out to open the car door for Lizzie. She waited, unsure she would be steady on her feet without his support.

"Welcome, my friends," boomed a jolly man as the couple entered.

"It's good to see you, Tony." Lizzie grinned at the owner, a burly man in his mid-fifties with thick brown hair and deep brown eyes.

"It's been too long. I hope everything is okay." Tony pulled Lizzie into a hug then slapped Ian on the back. "You don't look so good."

"It's been a crazy weekend," Ian said. Tony led them to a table by the window, yet far enough from the front door.

The scent of fresh bread made Lizzie's stomach rumble. "What's good today?" she asked.

"You know everything is always good," Tony said with a mock pout.

"Of course," Ian replied, "but today we want something special."

"Special, eh? What's the occasion?" Tony's eyes twinkled and Lizzie wondered if he'd already heard the news.

"We're getting married," Lizzie blurted out.

"Married! Wonderful, that is wonderful news." Tony clapped his hands. "I will bring you the best we have to offer." He hurried off to the kitchen, where cheers arose a minute later.

"I wish I could call Ron and Emma," Lizzie said, her happiness slipping at the thought of her friends.

"I know." Ian reached across the table and took her hand. "Can you send them a letter by Federal Express?"

Lizzie shook her head. "I don't know if FedEx goes to the village they are in."

"We'll find a way to let them know as soon as possible," Ian assured her. Lizzie squeezed his hand, knowing if there was a way, Ian would find it.

"Should we call your parents?"

"We'll call them this evening. I want to enjoy this moment alone with you."

"We aren't exactly alone," Lizzie said, glancing toward the kitchen door.

"Tony isn't going to disturb us. I love you so much, and I don't ever want you to be afraid. Promise you will tell me what's going on in that head of yours from now on."

Lizzie dropped her gaze to the table, expecting to feel a cloud of shame eclipsing her heart, but there was only peace. She looked up and met Ian's blue eyes. "I promise."

The kitchen door swung open and Tony emerged carrying a tray. Sizzling pans of steak fajitas were set before them.

"You didn't think I remembered your first meal here, did you?" Tony winked. "Now I will leave you two lovebirds alone. You know where I'll be if you need anything else."

"I told you Tony wouldn't disturb us," Ian said with a chuckle.

Lizzie shook her head and grinned. "He knows how to make an entrance."

Steam still rose from the fajita pans, but the sizzling had subsided. Lizzie reached for a tortilla and filled it with strips of steak, lettuce, tomato, cheese, and sour cream. "He even remembered I don't like guacamole."

"And that I do," Ian said, spooning it onto his own tortilla.

Lizzie made a face. "Don't expect me to kiss you after you eat that."

Ian leaned across the table. "Then kiss me now."

CHAPTER THIRTY EIGHT

"I'm not going to find anything more on these names." Stephen closed his laptop with a decisive snap and threw himself back on the couch. Upon learning of Jeffrey's accident and the canceled plans to attend Michelle's concert, Stephen had buried himself in work, searching for any information on the four remaining names on the Snowcap Lodge list. He'd only slept a couple of hours Saturday night, and now, with the sun setting on Sunday, he was ready to give up.

Snowcap and the resort in Boston were the smallest of the Ryland properties. The two hotels in Las Vegas had thousands of employees and Stephen hadn't received a list of questionable ones from them. He moved to the kitchen and found a bottle of Aspirin in a drawer. He popped a couple into his mouth and swallowed hard.

He removed his glasses and rubbed his tired eyes. "I need to get out of here."

He grabbed a pair of sneakers and stuffed his feet inside, collected his cell phone and keys, and stepped outside. The apartment complex was quiet for a Sunday afternoon and the fresh air helped sweep the cobwebs from his brain. He glanced toward the playground where half a dozen kids usually played, but it was deserted.

His cell phone rang as he stepped into his SUV. "Hello?"

"Steve-o, it's Jason. I have news for you."

"Already? That's great." Stephen settled into his seat but left the door open.

"Piece of cake. I'd been wanting to call this chick I worked with at Snowcap, but didn't have a real reason to. Thanks for giving me an in."

"Glad I could help," Stephen said. "What did you find out?"

"There's not much to say. They have all been reliable employees, no one has had any issues with them. Melissa, that's my friend, was surprised when I asked about them."

Stephen gripped the phone tighter. "You didn't say anything about the investigation did you?"

"Of course not. I told Melissa I'd been thinking about my time at Snowcap and was curious about who was still there. I asked about a bunch of people, not just your guys. I even asked if anyone might be looking to move on, that I might have some spots in my company."

"Do you?" Stephen asked.

"We're always hiring, but I don't have any input. Anyway, the point is, you can tell your boss these folks are okay. Kira on the other hand, I'll let you know more once I meet her, but Melissa was irritated when I mentioned Kira's name."

"Interesting. Any idea why?"

"Not exactly, but I like to think Melissa was jealous, afraid I may be interested in Kira."

"She's really going to think you're interested when she sees pictures of you and Kira at the McNally benefit."

"I don't think Kira's going to be posting any pictures of me. Have you seen her MySpace page recently? She's posted five different outfits she's considering for this thing."

"Designer outfits, I'm sure."

"Maybe, I don't know much about women's clothes."

"Thanks for the update, man. I'll have to find a way to hold Mr. Kingsley off until next week on Kira, but this other news should make him happy."

"I'll be in touch after the party. Until then, hang loose."

"Yeah, you too," Stephen said, not understanding what exactly that meant. He ended the call, dropped the phone into the center console, closed the door and buckled his seatbelt. Thank goodness LJ came through.

CHAPTER THIRTY NINE

Screeching metal followed by an explosion startled Michelle from a deep sleep. She sat up and looked around for the source of the noise, chuckling to herself when she saw the scene of a terrible wreck on the television. She'd fallen asleep to her favorite sitcom, but now an action thriller played.

After the concert the previous night, she and her bandmates had hit another club, then had breakfast at Denny's. She'd stumbled home at three in the morning and collapsed on the couch. She now reached for the remote and clicked the television off.

She stood and stretched her muscles, wrinkling her nose in disgust. Her clothes smelled of cigarette smoke and stale beer. She stripped them off on the way to the bathroom and stood under the hot water for several minutes until she felt fully awake. Twenty minutes later she stepped out of the steamy bathroom, wrapped in a thick bathrobe.

In the kitchen she perused the contents of the refrigerator; a bowl of soup covered with a thin film of congealed fat, a hunk of fuzzy cheese, a bag of salad with more brown than green leaves, half a gallon of milk that had expired a week earlier.

"I've got to stop eating out all the time," she murmured as she reached for the cordless phone.

"Hello?" she heard a voice say when she turned the phone on.

"Hello?" she replied.

"It's Jeffrey. I didn't even hear any ringing."

"I was calling to order a pizza," Michelle said.

"Great timing. I was calling to see if you wanted to get something to eat."

"I don't know." Michelle pulled the bathrobe tighter around her neck. "I'm kind of wiped after last night."

"No problem," Jeffrey said. "Did you have a good show?"

"I think it went well. How are you feeling?"

"I'm achy, but I'll survive. Sitting around the house is about to drive me crazy, though."

"I can come over if you want," Michelle offered, hoping he'd say no.

"That's okay. I'll order in some food and find a movie on TV. You get some rest."

"Are you sure?" Guilt swept through Michelle. He'd been in a wreck and here she was complaining about being tired because she'd chosen to stay out so late.

"We'll catch up another time."

"All right, thanks." Michelle hung up and leaned on the kitchen counter. Is it so wrong I want to chill out this afternoon, she thought. I work hard all week and need some downtime. She dialed the phone.

"I can bring over some pizza," she said when Jeffrey answered.

"You don't need to," Jeffrey said and she could hear his smile. "I understand you're tired. You're basically working two jobs and need some time to relax."

"I was thinking that too, but what's stopping me from relaxing with you?"

"Your choice. I'll be here all night."

"See you in a bit." Michelle put the phone down and made her way back to her bedroom. She chose and discarded a dozen shirts before choosing an ivory blouse and a pair of black corduroys. On the way out the door she placed an order for pick-up and headed for her favorite pizza joint.

CHAPTER FORTY

Orange and gold painted the sky as Michelle pulled into Jeffrey's driveway. The air was heavy with the scent of roses, but she didn't see any bushes nearby. She carried the pizza tucked between her hip and her arm, a two-liter bottle of Coke in the crook of her other arm. At the door she leaned forward, using her head to knock. She was preparing to knock again when the door swung open.

"Come in," Jeffrey said, reaching for the pizza.

Michelle stepped inside, closing the door behind her. "It's fortunate your wrist break was on the same side as the collarbone break."

"Yeah, I can't imagine not being able to use either arm. Good thing it's my left and not my right, too. I would be helpless if I couldn't use my right hand."

"I'm a lefty." Michelle lifted her left hand and waved.

"Then I recommend you don't get into car accidents." Jeffrey set the pizza on the table. "I'll get some paper plates and napkins. Have a seat."

"Let me help." Michelle followed him into the kitchen. It was small, just enough room for a refrigerator, sink, stove, and a couple of cabinets. She saw a roll of paper towels by the sink and reached for them while Jeffrey opened a cabinet door. He set two glasses on the counter before stepping to the refrigerator and pulling a pack of paper plates off the top.

Michelle handed him the paper towels and reached for the glasses. "I'll get some ice. You go sit down."

Jeffrey carried the plates and napkins back to the coffee table and settled himself on the couch. "What kind of movies do you like?" he asked.

Michelle set the glasses down and opened the bottle of Coke. "Comedies, just about anything with Johnny Depp, except, there was one, oh I can't remember the name, something about a gate. It was kind of creepy."

"*The Whole Nine Yards* is coming on soon. I think that's a comedy."

Michelle reached for a slice of pizza. "Yeah, with Bruce Willis and that guy from Friends. That sounds good."

Jeffrey changed the channel on the TV and turned the volume down. "I appreciate that you came over, but honestly, you didn't have to."

Michelle dabbed at some sauce at the corner of her mouth. "I know, but I really didn't need to eat a whole pizza by myself. This saves me half the calories."

Jeffrey laughed, folded his piece of pizza, and took a large bite. Michelle leaned back on the couch and munched on her crust.

"I think I owe Lizzie an apology," she said as she reached for another piece.

"Why?" Jeffrey wiped his fingers on his napkin and took a drink of his soda.

"I thought she was calling me to talk about religion and I wasn't very nice about it."

"She didn't mention it when she came over last night. I wouldn't worry about it."

Michelle's muscles tensed and her jaw tightened. "She was here last night?"

"Yeah, I mentioned how sick I was of watching Lifetime movies so she brought over some action flicks."

"I see." Michelle dropped her half-eaten pizza on her plate.

"What's wrong?" Jeffrey set his plate on the table.

"Nothing, I just," Michelle stood and reached for her purse. "I forgot I'm supposed to be working on a new song for the band."

"Michelle." Jeffrey reached for her hand, but she stepped away.

"I hope your bones heal quickly." She grasped the doorknob but it wouldn't turn.

"Don't go," Jeffrey said.

Michelle looked over her shoulder and saw Jeffrey coming toward her. She turned the knob again before realizing it was locked. Knowing Jeffrey would be beside her in a second, she looked back at the door, flipped the lock and pushed the door open.

"If you're working on a song, I understand, but if there's something bothering you..."

Michelle walked outside, leaving the door open. At her car, she turned to see him standing in the doorway. His brow furrowed and his mouth opened as if getting ready to speak. She ducked into her car and slammed the door. Jeffrey was still in the doorway when she pulled away.

CHAPTER FORTY ONE

Back at the church, Ian pulled into a spot next to Lizzie's old Camry.

"Let me make you dinner tonight." He slipped his hand from the gearshift to her knee.

Lizzie unfastened her seatbelt. "I'd like that. What time should I come over?"

"Six-thirty, then we can call my parents after we eat."

"You want me to bring anything?"

"Just your beautiful smile." He leaned over and cradled her head in his hand, his eyes piercing her with their intensity. She closed her own eyes and met his lips. When Ian pulled away, Lizzie kept her eyes closed for another heartbeat.

"I'm going to enjoy that for the rest of my life," she murmured.

"I hope so." Ian rubbed his thumb over her cheek before letting go.

Lizzie opened her door. "I'll see you at six-thirty."

She slipped out of her seat and pressed the door closed. Her hands were shaking when she went to unlock her car. She had to take a deep breath to steady herself. The sports car purred behind her and she knew Ian wouldn't leave until she was on her own way. The thought warmed her. She looked back after opening her door. Ian smiled and she waved then ducked into the car.

It took two attempts to get the Camry to sputter to life. Ian had never made her feel bad about her aging vehicle; even now, his sleek BMW beside her, she wasn't ashamed of her car. He was a good man.

She backed out and glided through the lot to the exit. Ian followed close behind. When she exited I-4 for downtown, she heard him toot his horn and checked the rearview mirror to see him waving as he passed.

The neighborhood was quiet when Lizzie coasted to a stop in front of her house. She hurried up the front steps and through the door, dropping her purse on a chair as she passed through to the kitchen. She rummaged through a drawer until she found a small box of notecards, which she carried back to the couch. Curling up with her feet underneath her and using a magazine from the coffee table for a writing surface, she began a note to Ron and Emma.

You won't believe what happened. Ian proposed today! I wish you were here so I could tell you all about it. I think I might burst with happiness. I promise a longer letter soon, but I just had to let you know.

She sealed the envelope, but hesitated addressing it. She reached for the phone and dialed Federal Express. When the automated system answered, she kept asking for an agent until a live person came on the line.

"I need to find out if you deliver to a particular address."

"Sure, I can check that for you. What is the address?"

Lizzie provided the one she had and waited with bated breath.

"I'm sorry, we don't show that as a valid address. Do you have another I can try?"

Lizzie exhaled. "No, not right now. Can you tell me if you deliver anywhere near that address?"

"No, we need an address to do a search."

"Okay, thank you."

"Thank you for calling Federal Express."

Lizzie hung up and dropped the phone on the couch. She had hours to kill before dinner. She tossed the envelope on the coffee table and stood, wandering to the window, then back to the kitchen, and finally to her bedroom. The bed looked inviting and she realized she wasn't restless, she was tired. She set her alarm clock for five o'clock, crawled in bed and pulled the comforter over her head.

CHAPTER FORTY TWO

The candles were lit, the table was set, a bouquet of flowers waited on the counter, and the pasta was boiling. Ian checked the recipe he'd printed off the Internet and found he had time to prepare the salads before it needed to be drained. He opened a bag of chopped lettuce and dumped it into a large bowl, to which he added chopped sweet peppers, cherry tomatoes, dried cranberries, shredded cheese, and herb-seasoned croutons. He used a pair of large spoons to toss the mixture together before covering the bowl and setting it in the refrigerator.

"Everything has to be perfect," he mumbled to himself as he checked the pasta. "A couple more minutes."

He checked the recipe again and gathered the rest of the ingredients, mixing them together, then poured everything into a baking dish and set the oven timer for twenty-five minutes.

Plenty of time to get a shower, he thought. He picked out a pair of dress pants and a nice shirt that he carried into the bathroom with him.

"Good heavens," he exclaimed upon seeing himself in the mirror. His shirt was wrinkled, he had a good start of a beard sprouting from his face, and deep purple bags made his eyes appear deeper set than normal. "I must have been quite a sight, proposing at the front of the church, looking like a hobo. I can't believe Lizzie accepted."

He turned on the shower, waiting until it was steaming hot before stepping under the spray. When he stepped out of the bathroom, the oven timer was ringing. He fastened the last button on his shirt as he moved into the kitchen and opened the oven door.

The cheese bubbled and the breadcrumbs were golden brown. He checked the clock; ten minutes before Lizzie should arrive. He covered the dish with aluminum foil, removed the salad from the refrigerator and placed it on the table with two bottles of salad dressing; a raspberry vinaigrette for Lizzie and Thousand Island for himself.

The candles had burned down almost a quarter of the way. "I shouldn't have lit them until now." He thought about changing them out, but a knock at the door stopped him.

CHAPTER FORTY THREE

When he opened the door, he couldn't breathe. Lizzie wore an aqua dress that managed to make her eyes bluer than he'd ever seen them. A string of pearls ringed her neck and matched the bunch dangling from her ears. Her curls floated around her face with an angelic effect.

"You look amazing," he breathed, reaching for her hand. He pulled her inside and closed the door.

"I wasn't sure what to wear." She ran a hand down the skirt of her dress.

"Would you like a glass of wine?" Ian hurried to the refrigerator.

Lizzie nodded and Ian poured two glasses. "Whatever you cooked smells delicious."

Ian brought the glasses to the table. "I thought we could start with a salad while the main course cools a bit." He pulled out a chair for her.

Lizzie served herself some salad and reached for the bottle of vinaigrette. "My favorite dressing."

"Only the best for you." Ian took his own seat and rubbed his hands on his pants, surprised at how sweaty his palms were. He filled his bowl with salad and drizzled dressing on it.

"Do you want to say a blessing?" Lizzie extended her hand across the table.

Ian twined his fingers with hers and closed his eyes. "Dear Lord, thank you for bringing Lizzie into my life, thank you for bringing us through the rough parts. I pray you will guide us through the days and years ahead. Bless this food, may it bring nourishment to our bodies, and not give us food poisoning. In your name I pray, Amen."

"Amen." Lizzie giggled. "I really hope we don't get food poisoning. Tomorrow's going to be a busy day at the hotel."

"I'm pretty sure we're safe, but a little extra precaution never hurts." Ian dug into his salad.

They ate in silence for several minutes, Ian watching Lizzie spear a piece of lettuce, half a tomato, a cranberry and a bit of crouton, placing it in her mouth with delicate grace.

Lizzie broke the silence as she speared her last bite of salad. "I called FedEx and they don't deliver to the village Ron and Emma are working in."

"I'm sorry. I know how important it is to you. Maybe tomorrow you can contact the organization they are working with and see if they have a way to get in touch with them."

"Of course, why didn't I think of that?"

"I'm sure you would have once you had a chance to think about it." Ian stood. "May I clear your bowl?"

Lizzie handed him the empty bowl and raised her napkin to her lips. Ian tucked the bowls into the dishwasher before uncovering the pasta and dishing it out onto two plates.

"Careful, it's still hot," he warned when he set the plate in front of her.

"It looks wonderful. What's it called?" Lizzie leaned forward and inhaled the aroma.

"Fontina and Mascarpone baked pasta." Ian returned to his seat.

"Mmm," Lizzie sighed in approval after taking her first bite.

Ian scooped up some penne, making sure he got plenty of cheese. "Not bad for my first try."

"You can cook like this for me anytime."

"I'm going to hold you to that." Ian winked at her.

"Did your mom give you the recipe?"

"No, I found it online. I remembered you talking about a recipe you'd seen that called for fontina cheese. I couldn't remember where you saw it, so I did a Google search for fontina cheese recipes, this was one of the first to come up."

"Impressive. What other talents have you been hiding from me?"

Ian shrugged. "I guess you'll just have to wait and see. Do you want seconds?"

"Depends on what you have for dessert."

Ian stood and cleared the plates. "I won't ever compete with your baking skills, so I only have this." He returned to the table with a Pepperidge Farm chocolate cake.

"Frozen cake!" Lizzie clapped her hands. "You know me so well."

"I like to think so." Ian cut her a piece and placed it on a small plate. He bent down and kissed her cheek after setting the plate before her.

"Did you really plan to propose while we were in Vermont?" Lizzie asked before taking a bite of the cake.

"I carried the ring with me everywhere we went. This past Friday was the first time I haven't had that box in my pocket for the past two and a half months."

Lizzie's fork stopped mid-way to her mouth. She lowered it to the plate, her eyes wide with disbelief. "No you didn't."

"I did. There's probably a bruise on my thigh from all the times I had to carry it in my pant's pocket because I wasn't wearing a jacket. Speaking of which," he stood and crossed to the kitchen bar where he collected a bouquet of flowers. "I forgot to give you these."

Lizzie reached up and took the bouquet, gasping when she saw the ring tied around the center flower. "Ian, it's stunning."

Two platinum bands encrusted with diamonds crossed in an "S" pattern, wrapping around a caret diamond flanked by sapphires. He reached over and pulled the ribbon loose, letting the ring drop into his palm. Lizzie's hand was shaking when he took it, lifted it to his lips and kissed it before slipping the ring onto her finger. "Now it's official."

Lizzie threw her arms around his neck. "Thank you for loving me."

Ian stroked the back of her hair, breathing in the scent of her perfume. He savored the feel of her heart pounding against his chest. "I'll never stop loving you."

CHAPTER FORTY FOUR

"What was that all about?" Jeffrey grumbled as he closed the door. He shuffled back to the couch and reached for another piece of pizza. "I guess I can look for something more exciting to watch."

He flipped through the channels hoping to find an action movie or at least a good cop drama, but every channel seemed to be playing romance movies or sitcoms. You'd think this was Valentine's weekend, he thought as he clicked off the television. He devoured two more pieces of pizza and half the bottle of Coke before taking the leftovers to the kitchen.

His cell phone rang and he groaned when he read the caller ID. "Hi, mom" he answered.

"How are you doing, sweetie. Do you need anything?"

"I'm fine, just finished eating."

"Are you keeping your arm immobilized like the doctor told you?"

"Yes, I'm wearing the sling right now." Jeffrey adjusted his arm in the sling as if his mother could see it.

"Have you been putting ice on it?"

"Mom, I'm a grown man, I can take care of myself."

"I know, but I still worry about you."

He moved into his bedroom and stretched out on the bed. "I am kind of bored. Being alone is easier when I'm not injured."

"You know you are welcome to come home anytime."

"I just wish I had more friends. I can't expect Lizzie to be at my side every time I need help."

"What about the young lady who brought you home from the hospital? What was her name?"

"Michelle. She came by, but took off after only a few minutes, like I spooked her or something. I don't know what her deal is."

"She obviously cares enough to visit you in the hospital and even to come by your house."

"Yeah, it's complicated. I wish I knew some of the people at church better. I don't feel like I can call any of them out of the blue just to talk."

"Why don't you take a couple days off work and come stay with us. I can make sure your collarbone stays iced and we can rent movies, maybe even play Scrabble. Remember when we'd do that when you were little?"

Jeffrey smiled at the memory. The two had spent many evenings together while his father worked late or traveled. Even as a ten-year-old he'd been good with words and often beat his mother at the game.

"I don't think I can take any time off right now. We had to change plumbing contractors and the new guys start tomorrow."

"Don't you have a foreman who can oversee that?"

Jeffrey mulled over the idea, his shoulder beginning to throb again. "I'll think about it."

"That's all I ask," his mother said. "Now go put some ice on that shoulder."

"On my way to the kitchen now," he said as he sat up. "Thanks for calling, mom."

"Good night, honey. I love you."

"You too." Jeffrey stuffed the phone in his pocket and made his way to the kitchen where he pulled an ice pack from the freezer. He wrapped it in a dishtowel and returned to the living room, settling on the couch before placing the pack on his shoulder. He winced at the cold, but soon the area grew numb and the pain subsided.

CHAPTER FORTY FIVE

When the table was cleared, the kitchen cleaned, and the candles nearly burned out, Ian led Lizzie into the room he used as an office and opened his computer.

"What are we doing?" Lizzie asked.

"Calling my parents," he replied as he typed on the keyboard. A minute later a video image of Colin and Cassandra Cavanaugh appeared on the computer screen. "Hi." Ian waved at his parents.

"It's good to see you," Colin said.

"What's this all about?" Cassandra asked.

Ian scooted his chair back and motioned for Lizzie to move her chair closer. "Lizzie and I have some news for you."

Ian saw his mother reach for his father's hand. He reached for Lizzie's as well and gave it a squeeze. "We're getting married," he announced.

Cassandra squealed with delight and Colin nodded, a wide grin filling his face. "We're so happy for both of you," he said.

"Welcome to the family, Lizzie." Cassandra swatted at tears spilling from the corner of her eyes.

Ian exchanged a look with his mother and she blew him a kiss.

"Have you talked about a date yet?" Colin asked.

"No, we haven't had a chance." Ian looked to Lizzie. "Do you have any preference?"

"I want to do it as soon as possible, but I can't imagine not having Ron and Emma at the ceremony."

"When do they come back from Kenya?" Cassandra asked.

"Not until August, and I don't know what's going to be happening at work with the buyout." Lizzie bit her lip.

"Planning a wedding can take a lot of time. If there is anything we can do to help, you'll let us know won't you?" Cassandra asked.

"Thanks, mom."

Lizzie looked at Ian and he could see the wheels spinning behind her eyes. "Where are we going to have the wedding? Your family is all in Connecticut. My extended family is in North Carolina. There aren't too many people here who I'd want to invite."

"Slow down." Ian placed a finger over her lips. "We don't have to make any decisions right now."

Cassandra and Colin chuckled. "Wherever and whenever, you know we'll be there," Colin said.

"Let me see the ring," Cassandra said, leaning closer to the computer.

Lizzie held up her hand, smiling when Cassandra whispered, "That is lovely."

"Nicely done, son," Colin agreed.

"I'm so happy you told us to have the video conference on tonight. I can't imagine not having seen your faces." Cassandra reached out and touched the computer.

"I wanted to make tonight special for us all," Ian said.

"I wish you could conference Ron and Emma as well." Cassandra gave Lizzie a sympathetic look.

"If they had an Internet connection out there, I'm sure Ian would find a way, but Federal Express says they can't even locate the village they are working in."

"We'll get in touch with them as soon as we can," Ian assured them.

"Show me the ring again, one more time before we hang up," Cassandra said.

Lizzie laughed and raised her hand to the camera again.

"I love you guys," Ian said.

"We love you too. Congratulations," Colin said.

"We'll talk soon."

"Good night." Cassandra waved then the picture disappeared.

"That was wonderful. How did you do it?" Lizzie asked.

"We both purchased the software a few weeks ago for work. Dad and I used it once to test it out. I knew if we ever got engaged I would have this to let them know."

Lizzie kissed his hand, then his wrist, and moved up his arm until she reached his neck. She slid from her chair into his lap and rested her head on his shoulder. "We're going to have a perfect life aren't we?"

"I can't promise perfect, but I promise as close to it as possible."

CHAPTER FORTY SIX

"What in the world happened to you?" Jenny exclaimed as Jeffrey stepped inside the office Monday morning.

"I was in an accident Friday night," Jeffrey replied.

Jenny scrambled to her boss' side and took the briefcase that dangled from his good hand. "Sit down. What can I get for you?"

Jeffrey sank into his chair. "A cup of coffee would be a good start."

"Of course." Jenny scooted across the room to the coffee pot and filled a tall mug.

Jeffrey took the cup and nodded for Jenny to sit down. "The new plumbers are supposed to start today. Have you seen any of them?"

"Not yet, but it's early."

"I don't have any meetings this week, do I?"

"No, your calendar is clear for the next couple of weeks."

"Good, I think I'm going to take a couple days off." Jeffrey grimaced. "Well, not completely off. I'll take my laptop and catch up on paperwork. If anything comes up, you can call me."

"Do you want me to keep you updated on the progress of the new plumbers?"

"I'd appreciate that." Jeffrey took a sip of his coffee and thought about the men working for him. "Has Donald come in yet?"

"No, sir. Only a handful of guys have checked in." Jenny glanced at the clock. "They should start pouring in any minute, though."

"Once everyone is here, I'll set the goals for the week and let them know Donald is in charge while I'm gone."

The trailer door opened and six guys stepped inside. Jeffrey watched as they found their time cards and punched in.

"Morning, boss. Looks like you had quite a weekend," one of the guys joked as he poured a cup of coffee.

"You should see the other guy," Jeffrey said. The office was now alive with men streaming in and out. "Donald, hang back a minute," Jeffrey called when the site foreman had punched his card.

"What's up?" Donald asked. His grey eyes sized up Jeffrey's cast and sling.

"I'm leaving you in charge for a few days. I want you to keep a close eye on the new plumbers. If they aren't cutting it, then I want to know. Give Jenny a report each evening before you leave."

"Yes, sir. I appreciate your confidence in me."

"Gather the men and I'll be out to address them in a minute."

Donald stood and put his hard hat on. "Right away."

"Would you mind gathering up any of the paperwork I need to go through and put it along with my laptop in my briefcase?" Jeffrey asked.

Jenny raised a folder. "Already on it."

"What would I do without you, Jenny?"

"Remember that when this project is completed and you move on to even bigger things."

Jeffrey chuckled. "I don't know if I want anything bigger than this."

"What you want and what you deserve to be given can be two different things. Now get out there and lay down the law so you can go home."

"On my way." Jeffrey stood up and shuffled out the door.

It was a beautiful day, clear blue sky, no wind and the temperature hovering around seventy-five. Jeffrey stood on the top step surveying the construction site. Donald had gathered most of the men, but a few stragglers still shuffled in from their cars.

"Hustle up," Jeffrey called to them as he descended the stairs. He scanned the crowd for new faces, and found a knot of men at the edge of the circle that had gathered. When he saw the stragglers come out of the trailer, Jeffrey whistled loudly, getting everyone's attention.

"As you can see, I had a bit of an accident over the weekend. I'm going to spend a couple of days at home, catching up on paperwork. That doesn't mean I don't have eyes everywhere. If anyone is slacking off, I'll know. Donald is going to be in charge while I'm off-site." Jeffrey turned his attention to the new plumbers.

"We've got some new faces this week. I want you to make them feel welcome, but I also want the plumbing back on track. We have an inspection in ten days and I can't ask for an extension." Jeffrey paused and allowed his eyes to wander over the men, looking for any signs of trouble. "That's all. Now get to work and have a safe day."

The crowd dispersed and Jeffrey could hear team leaders calling out orders. He watched until everyone seemed to be on task, then returned to the office. He wobbled for several seconds before catching the edge of a desk for balance.

"You better sit down," Jenny said as she hurried to his side.

"The doctor said I might experience some dizziness from the concussion." Jeffrey accepted Jenny's assistance to his chair. "It will pass."

"Are you going to be okay to drive home?"

"I took a taxi in. I haven't had a chance to get a rental car yet."

"I can take you home. The office will be fine for half an hour."

Jeffrey closed his eyes and let his head rest against the back of the chair. "Just call me a taxi."

"Are you sure? It's not a problem."

"I need a few minutes to collect myself. By the time a taxi gets here I should be fine. I guess I overestimated my strength."

"All right," Jenny replied, but Jeffrey could tell by the way she drew out the words she wasn't happy with his choice.

"I need you here keeping an eye on everything," Jeffrey said. "You can either call or email me at the end of the day, whichever is easier for you."

Jeffrey opened his eyes and met his assistance's stare. "I'm going to be fine."

She tried to smile, but Jeffrey could see the concern in her eyes. After placing a call to the taxi service, she busied herself straightening papers on her desk and rearranging pens in a cup.

A car horn sounded and Jenny was by Jeffrey's side before he moved in his chair. She snatched his briefcase off the desk with one hand and used the other to help Jeffrey to his feet. They crossed the narrow trailer together and Jenny held the door open for him, then followed him down the stairs.

Jeffrey took another look at the construction site before opening the car door and ducking inside. The men were working and no one seemed to notice his departure. Jenny laid the briefcase on his lap.

"I'm only a phone call away if anything comes up," Jeffrey said.

"We can hold down the fort for a few days." Jenny smiled and closed the door.

Jeffrey gave the cab driver an address and closed his eyes.

CHAPTER FORTY SEVEN

A blue jay squawked at Lizzie as she stepped out of her car. She hurried up the ramp of the hotel loading bay and pushed through the doors into a service corridor.

"Good morning," called a bright-faced housekeeper as she passed by pushing a laundry cart.

"Morning," Lizzie replied as she sped down the hallway, pausing only when she reached the door that would put her in the lobby. She took a minute to catch her breath and ran a hand down her skirt to make sure it hadn't bunched up on her. Satisfied she was presentable, she stepped through the door and crossed the lobby with long, measured steps. She smiled at the few guests milling about.

The door to the front office opened and Stephen stood in the doorway. He stepped back as she approached. "I was getting worried about you," he said.

"I'm only five minutes late," Lizzie said. Stephen followed her into her office.

"You're usually here before anyone else on the day shift. Is everything all right?"

Lizzie dropped her purse on her desk and pressed the button to turn on her computer. "Everything's fine. I just forgot to turn my alarm on last night."

Stephen leaned on the back of her guest chair. "That's not like you."

Lizzie looked up at her friend and felt a crush of guilt at the concern she saw in his eyes. "It was a kind of crazy weekend." She fiddled with the zipper on her purse then extended her left hand, palm down. When Stephen didn't take his eyes off her face she shook her hand a bit. Finally, Stephen looked down and she watched his eyes widen. He looked back at her, his mouth agape.

"Is that what I think it is?"

Lizzie nodded. "We got engaged yesterday. Can you believe it?"

Stephen stepped around the chair then the desk and pulled Lizzie into a fierce hug. "It's about time," he said.

Lizzie giggled. "It's not like we've been dating for years."

Stephen released her and took a seat. "No you haven't, but it's obvious how crazy about you he is."

Lizzie settled into her chair and twisted the ring on her finger. "It feels so strange."

"You're happy, right?" Stephen leaned forward and placed a hand on the desk.

"Of course I am." Lizzie sighed. "For the first time in a really long time I feel like," she paused, searching for the right word, "I don't know, like my life is in balance again."

"Congratulations, Lizzie. You deserve to be happy." Stephen stood. "I was getting ready to send my report to Mr. Kingsley on the Snowcap Lodge employees. You want me to copy you in on it?"

"You're done already?" Lizzie looked up in surprise.

"I'm still looking into the one girl I told you about, but I have a friend in Colorado. We talked over the weekend. He worked at Snowcap for a few months and still had contacts there. He said the other names on the list were unremarkable, which matches everything I could find on them." Stephen grinned. "As for Kira, my friend has a date with her on Friday. I should know her whole story by the end of the night."

"You trust this friend?"

"Yeah, we went to college together. He's a good guy."

"I'm sure Mr. Kingsley will be impressed. No need to copy me in, though, this is your gig, but you might include Cynthia in HR."

"Already on it. I'm worried about the Vegas resorts, though. What if there are a lot of people he wants me to look into?"

"You'll do fine. You've proven your resourcefulness."

"I don't know anyone in Vegas. Without Jason I'd still be banging my head against the wall with those other names."

"Don't worry about it until Mr. Kingsley gives you more information. Maybe these background checks will be all he needs. I imagine the employees in Vegas are screened pretty well, considering the amount of money that flows through."

Stephen didn't look convinced, but Lizzie noticed his jaw relax. "I hope you're right."

"It's all going to work out. You'll see."

Stephen moved to the door. "I'll let you get to work. Our first concierge guest is scheduled to arrive at two this afternoon."

"Who's working the evening shift?"

"Jessica. Ben has the week off."

"That's right." Lizzie shook her head. "Do you need any help getting arrival packets ready?"

"I'm good. I just have to print out itineraries."

"All right. Let me know if you need anything. I have a meeting at noon to go over the convention calendar."

Stephen nodded and closed the door behind him, leaving Lizzie alone in the quiet office. She looked at the ring on her finger for several minutes. I have to find a way to tell Ron and Emma, she thought. She turned her attention to her computer and opened her Internet browser, then typed "International Mission Board". When a page of search results appeared, she found their website and navigated until finding a contact page. She reached for her phone and dialed the toll free number.

CHAPTER FORTY EIGHT

"Good morning," Ian sang out the greeting as he opened the office door.

"Good morning indeed. We've had a break in," Sheila grumbled.

"Are you sure? Have you called the police? Is anything missing?" Ian's mood changed instantly. "Are you okay?" he asked, reaching out to place a hand on her shoulder.

"One question at a time. I'm fine, I haven't called the police yet, and I don't know if anything is missing. Your office is a mess, though."

Ian looked through its open door. Papers were strewn all over the floor, desk, and drafting table. A chair was overturned and a coffee mug had been tipped over, spilling its contents onto a pile of magazines.

"Oh, Sheila, I'm so sorry." Ian leaned against her desk. "We haven't been robbed. That was all me."

"What do you mean?" Sheila's eyes narrowed.

"Maybe we should sit down and have some coffee."

Sheila led the way into the kitchen where she'd already set out two mugs. The coffee pot gave a gurgle, spurt, and sigh, signaling brewing was complete. Sheila filled the cups and handed one to Ian before sitting down at a small table.

Ian leaned against the counter and took a sip of the hot coffee. He set the cup down and took a seat across from Sheila. "I came in late Friday. Lizzie and I, we didn't exactly have a fight, but I was angry."

He filled Sheila in on Jeffrey's accident, and the trip to the hospital. "I fell asleep here. When she called on Saturday, I lost it. I vaguely remember swiping at the sketches on the drafting table before I left. I didn't realize I'd made such a mess. I'm sorry."

Sheila's face softened. "Have you spoken with Lizzie?"

Ian suppressed the smile that tried to illuminate his face. "I did a lot of thinking and God did some work in my heart. I found her at church,

Sunday." He paused, knowing it would make Sheila crazy. She was leaning forward, attentive to his every word.

"And?" she finally had to ask.

"And," Ian allowed the smile to burst forth. "We're getting married."

A hand flew to Sheila's mouth and he could see tears forming in her eyes. "Really?" she whispered.

"Yep, we told my parents last night."

Sheila jumped up and waved her hand for Ian to do the same. He stood and hugged her, laughing when she punched his chest. "I was so sure you were going to tell me you two had broken up," she said.

Ian sobered. "The thought did cross my mind several times over the weekend."

"God has a beautiful plan for your lives, I know it." Sheila sighed. "I guess it's a good thing I hadn't called the police yet."

Ian nodded. "It would have been embarrassing to explain I had a temper tantrum and caused the mess myself."

"You better get in there and clean it up now. The mall developers will be here at ten."

"You're right." Ian grabbed his coffee cup and strolled back to his office. He found a clear spot on his desk to set the cup then started the task of collecting the scattered papers. He heard Sheila humming and turned to find her sopping up the spilled coffee and gathering the wet magazines.

"I'll see if any of them can be salvaged," she offered.

"Thanks." It took less than twenty minutes to clean up and get the mall plans ready for presentation. Ian dropped into his chair and reached for his coffee cup. The liquid was tepid, but he drank it down anyway. The clock read nine forty-seven. Plenty of time to check email, he thought, clicking on the mail icon. There were only four new messages, which he read through quickly, shooting off replies as needed.

A knocked sounded on his door and Sheila pushed it open. "The developers are here."

Ian stood and moved from behind the desk to meet his guests. Two men in dark suits entered. "Larry, Dan, it's good to see you." Ian extended his hand to each man.

"We're excited to see what you've come up with," Larry said.

Ian led them to the drafting table and removed the blank page that covered the plan he'd designed for the shopping center. Larry and Dan stepped closer, leaning in for a better view. Ian gave them a couple of minutes to inspect his work before speaking.

"I know you didn't ask for a parking garage, but I was reminded of something my fiancée said." He couldn't help smiling at the word. "She said she hates having to park on the other side of a shopping center from the one store she is there for. The garage triples the available spots close to each of the large retailers as well as the smaller shops nearby. Plus there is the added bonus of covered walkways for those rainy days that deter many shoppers."

Dan rubbed his chin and stepped back, taking in the plan from a distance. "I like the theory, but I'm not sure about the placement. The way it's drawn here, people driving by can't see all the stores that are available."

"We always planned to have a sign out front listing the main retailers," Larry said. "Maybe we could use a color code in the garage along with signs to help shoppers know where to park to be close to their favorite store."

"I like that," Dan said. "I also like how you've landscaped the walkways. Maybe we could use landscaping to help differentiate the parking zones as well."

"Something to think about. I don't think we want to overload shoppers with too many things to remember. I have a hard enough time remembering where I parked at the airport, was it turtle or beaver, level five?"

All three men laughed. "I think the color coding idea is great. Maybe use the anchor store's signature colors for that section, red for Target, blue for Old Navy, and so on."

"I like the way you think, Cavanaugh," Larry said.

"Is there anything else you would like adjusted?" Ian asked.

Larry looked to Dan who shook his head. "Looks good to me. Can we get some copies to share with the rest of the team?"

"Of course. I can have them delivered to you by Wednesday."

"Sounds good." Larry rapped the drafting table with his knuckles. "It's been a pleasure working with you on this project."

"Thank you, sir. When do you think you will break ground?"

"We don't have a firm date yet," Larry said.

"I'd like to see us get started before the end of summer," Dan said.

"I'll get you those copies, and if you need any changes made, you let me know."

"Thanks so much." Larry extended his hand and Ian shook it. Larry and Dan turned to leave. Sheila opened the door for them and Ian watched them leave before returning to his desk.

"They looked pleased," Sheila said when the door closed behind them.

"They were. Now I need to get the plans into the computer and send them copies."

"Do you want me to hold your calls?"

"I don't expect many, but if you could for the next couple of hours, that would be great."

"You got it." Sheila stepped back and closed his office door.

Ian turned his attention to his computer and started working.

CHAPTER FORTY NINE

"How was your show?"

Michelle looked up from her computer and saw her friend Wendy leaning against the cubicle wall. Even though the girl was slender, the wall shifted with her weight. The whole office was a maze of dominoes waiting for the right push.

"It was really good."

"Sorry I couldn't make it. My family's in town for the next week." Wendy wrinkled her nose.

"Are they staying with you?"

"No, thank heavens. They have a timeshare in Vegas and were able to trade out their points for a place here."

"It can't be that bad then. You only have to see them for a couple of hours each night, right?"

Wendy sighed. "They landed early Saturday and then I had to go with them to the theme parks on Sunday. I'm happy to be at work to have some quiet time."

"How old are your niece and nephew now?"

"Eleven and nine. My sister is in for some tough times. My niece is already acting like a teenager. I forgot how much drama teens can cause."

Michelle laid down her pen with a sigh and shifted in her chair. "Does the drama ever end?"

"Uh-oh, what happened?" Wendy moved to the chair by the cubicle wall and sat down.

"Jeffrey was supposed to come to the show, but he was in a wreck Friday night."

"Is he okay?"

"Yeah, he has some broken bones, but nothing serious. Anyway, he had his friend Lizzie call to tell me he wouldn't be at the show. I got kind of freaked when she called, thinking he'd told her to try to talk some sense into me about this whole God thing and I wasn't very nice to her."

"I'm sure you weren't that bad."

Michelle shrugged "I took a pizza to his place last night. When I told him how I'd reacted, he told me not to worry about it, she hadn't even mentioned it to him. I guess she went to his place Saturday night to keep him company. When he said that, I had to get out of there. I gave him some lame excuse about needing to work on a new song for the band."

Wendy drummed her fingers on her knee. Michelle waited for her friend to say something.

"Were you jealous?" Wendy finally asked.

Michelle shook her head. "No way. That's not possible."

"Are you sure?" Wendy's eyes crinkled around the edges and the corner of her lips twitched.

"We're just friends. He hasn't given any indication that he's interested in more than that."

"That doesn't mean you aren't interested in more. You mention him almost every day."

"I do not. I've only seen him a few times in the past three months."

Wendy shrugged and stood. "It's something to think about. He sounds like a decent guy."

Michelle couldn't dispute that. Despite her previous impression of him, Jeffrey had proven to be kind and honest.

"You want to go out for lunch, maybe around one?" Wendy asked.

"Hmm?" Michelle turned to her friend who had moved to the cubicle entrance.

"Lunch?"

"Rain check? I have a couple of deadlines coming up this week."

"No problem. Tell Jeffrey I said hello when you talk to him again." Wendy winked and strolled out of sight.

CHAPTER FIFTY

"Here you go, buddy," the cabby said, pulling to a stop.

Jeffrey opened his eyes and turned his head to look out the window. The car was parked in front of a large brick house with white columns and an oversized oak door. He reached for his wallet and handed the driver some bills.

"Keep the change," he said as he opened the door.

"Thanks, buddy."

Jeffrey slid out of the car, dragging the briefcase behind him. He steadied himself on the car door for a second before closing it and taking a step onto the fresh-cut lawn. He reached the sidewalk and looked to the left where the driveway arched away from the road toward the house. He shook his throbbing head and crossed the grass, stumbling when he reached the pad of concrete outside the front door. He leaned heavily against one of the flanking columns, the doorbell just beyond his reach.

Once he regained his balance, he moved forward and pressed the doorbell. He waited then pressed it again. The door opened to reveal Jacquelyn Robbins. Jeffrey didn't wait for her to greet him, but stepped forward, and reached for her arm.

"I need to sit down," he said.

Jacquelyn took the briefcase, wrapped an arm around Jeffrey's waist, and led him into the living room. She helped him down onto a couch, a groan of pain escaping him when she lifted his injured arm too high.

"I'm sorry. Let me get you some ice."

"Some ibuprofen would be good too," he croaked.

"I'll be right back."

Jeffrey kicked off his shoes and stretched out on the couch, gnashing his teeth against the pain in his head and shoulder. Jacquelyn returned before he'd found a comfortable position and he sat up to take the pills, accepting the glass of water she provided.

"Lay back and I'll put the ice pack on for you."

Jeffrey started to protest then let out a long sigh and lowered his head onto a cushion she had repositioned for him. He pointed to the spot where the pain was greatest and watched her apply the ice pack.

"Do you need anything else?"

"Not right now, just rest." Jeffrey closed his eyes. "Any word on my truck?"

"Your father called this morning. The yard it was towed to was closed over the weekend. They said it's in pretty bad shape. He went out to get some photos for your insurance."

"I need to arrange for a rental car."

"Worry about that tomorrow. You take a nap, and when you wake up I'll make you something to eat."

Jeffrey nodded. He felt the couch shift as Jacquelyn stood. Her footsteps were barely audible on the plush carpet, but Jeffrey could tell when she paused before turning down the hall toward the library. The ice started working to numb the pain in his shoulder and he began to breathe easier.

CHAPTER FIFTY ONE

A dull ache had started at Lizzie's temples. She turned off the computer monitor and pushed back from her desk, stretching her arms over her head as the chair rolled backward. A knock sounded on her door before Stephen opened it and leaned in, one hand holding onto the doorframe.

"I'm heading out," he said. "Jessica has the files on the four families scheduled to arrive this evening."

"Did you hear anything back from Mr. Kingsley?" Lizzie stood and crossed the small office so she was standing only a couple of feet from Stephen.

He looked over his shoulder before moving closer. "You were right. He doesn't have any concerns about the Vegas properties and only gave me two names in Boston," he whispered.

"Two names should be a breeze for you." Lizzie gave him a reassuring smile.

"I'll check for any MySpace profiles tonight."

"No, you won't. You did too much over the weekend without getting paid for it. Tonight, you're going home and forgetting all about work. Any profiles they may have will be waiting for you in the morning."

"It's no problem to look them up at home. I don't have anything else going on."

"Then it's time you found some hobbies." Lizzie reached for a worn book on a nearby filing cabinet. "Here, finish these crosswords."

Stephen took the book and flipped through it. There were dozens of crossword puzzles already completed.

"I started doing them after I came back from Vermont to make me stop thinking about work. After a week I lost interest."

"You did all of these in a week?"

Lizzie shrugged. "I'm pretty much always thinking about this place."

"That's going to change now you have a wedding to plan."

"Maybe we should just have the wedding here and I can do all the planning on company time."

Stephen laughed. Lizzie had said it as a joke, but when she heard it, she realized it wasn't such a bad idea.

"You aren't serious, are you?" Stephen sobered.

"I wasn't, but it does make sense." Lizzie glanced to her right where a dry erase calendar hung, showing the events planned at the hotel. She took a step toward it, her finger tapping her cheek as she studied the dates. A hand descending on her shoulder broke her concentration.

Stephen turned her to face him. "If you want to have the wedding here, then I'll support you, but if you are thinking of it only because it would be convenient, then I'll do everything I can to stop you."

"We've done some lovely weddings here," Lizzie protested.

"Yes, we have, but you know what made them so nice?" Stephen didn't wait for Lizzie to answer. "What made them nice was all the work you and Tammy put into them. Remember the wedding we had during Hurricane Charley? The power was out but you transformed the conference room into a magical place. If something like that happens during your wedding, do you think you will be able to sit back and let Tammy deal with it alone?"

Lizzie twirled a lock of hair around her finger. Stephen had a good point. Could she be both bride and wedding planner in her own hotel? She'd want to be in the kitchen checking on the food and overseeing the decorations.

"Maybe you're right," she conceded.

"Good," Stephen nodded. "Now I promise not to do any research tonight, if you promise to go home and forget about this place for the next twelve hours."

"Deal." Lizzie moved to her desk and retrieved her purse from the bottom drawer. "Let's go."

They crossed the lobby, which was oddly quiet for the dinner hour, and were halfway down the service corridor when Lizzie's phone rang.

"It's Tammy," she said. "You go on. I'll pop in her office and see what she needs."

Stephen gave her a stern look. "No wedding planning."

"You've convinced me. Don't worry." Lizzie bumped him playfully with her shoulder.

"All right. See you tomorrow."

Stephen turned left toward the loading bay door and Lizzie turned right. Tammy's office door was open so Lizzie didn't bother knocking.

"You rang?" Lizzie said when she entered the small yet airy office. A desk, two filing cabinets, and three chairs were its only furniture. Tammy was a fanatic about keeping the room clutter-free.

Tammy looked up, her eyes tired and heavy. "You didn't have to come down here."

"I was on my way out. What's up?"

Tammy looked at her watch then rubbed at the back of her neck. "I didn't realize it was so late. Go on home, we can talk tomorrow."

Lizzie plopped down into one of the chairs facing Tammy's desk. "I'm here now, let's have it."

Tammy sighed and slumped back in her chair. "My mom fell and broke her hip. She needs someone to take care of her and of course my dear brother is too busy traveling the world."

"Oh, Tammy. I'm so sorry. Is she going to be okay?" Lizzie leaned forward in her seat.

"The doctor said it was a clean break and there weren't any other injuries. She can't travel, though, so I have to go to Texas to care for her."

"I can handle things here. You need to be with your mom."

"Thanks, Lizzie. I know how busy you've been since the promotion."

"For the most part it's meetings that, frankly, I could care less about." Lizzie grimaced. "I almost wish I hadn't gotten the promotion."

"I know what you mean. Management is less managing and more meeting." Tammy chuckled and Lizzie was pleased to see a flash of humor in her friend's eyes.

"When do you think you'll be leaving?" Lizzie asked.

"I'll check on flights tonight. I can't imagine how expensive they are going to be with such short notice. Do you have time tomorrow to meet so I can catch you up on what's going on?"

"I'll make time. Call me in the morning."

CHAPTER FIFTY TWO

The smell of hamburgers teased Jeffrey from a deep sleep. He sniffed and detected the scent of french fries as well. His eyes fluttered open and he recognized the living room of his parents' house. The sight didn't match the smell, which he now recognized was take-out from Cheeburger Cheeburger, one of his favorite burger joints. He couldn't picture his cultured parents ever stepping foot in the restaurant.

Jacquelyn Robbins entered the library, the epitome of upper-class elegance in her perfectly pressed pants, wrinkle-free blouse, and the string of pearls he doubted she ever took off. Jeffrey tried to picture her walking into the vintage diner with its neon pink lighting and vinyl chairs.

"We picked up some burgers. I hope you're hungry." Jacquelyn bent to help Jeffrey get up from the couch.

"They smell great," Jeffrey said.

"Lizzie called to check on you and she mentioned Cheeburger Cheeburger was one of your favorite places. I thought a little comfort food might make you feel better."

Jeffrey took a minute to gain his footing, then followed his mother into the kitchen. Edward Robbins was already seated at the table, holding a cheeseburger.

"This is the best burger I've ever had," Edward said.

"Enjoy it now, because you won't be getting another any time soon," Jacquelyn chided. "Your doctor would have a fit if he saw you eating that."

Jeffrey sat down and Jacquelyn placed a burger in front of him. A plate piled high with french fries and onion rings sat in the middle of the table. Edward snatched a couple of fries and downed them with a smile. Jeffrey looked to his mother's place at the table and found she had cut her burger into quarters and placed it on a china plate. The scene was so ridiculous he wondered if he was still asleep and this was all a dream.

"Are you guys feeling all right?" Jeffrey asked.

"Fit as a fiddle," Edward said, lifting his burger once more.

"Do you want me to cut your burger up?" Jacquelyn reached toward the sandwich still in its wrapping.

Jeffrey covered it with his hand. "No, this is fine."

"He's no sissy," Edward scolded his wife. Mayonnaise, mustard, and burger juice ran between his fingers when he lifted the bun to his mouth.

Jeffrey shook his head in disbelief and unwrapped his own burger. The bun was still warm. He took a bite and groaned with delight. Forget everything else; this truly was his favorite meal.

"Edward, you've had enough fries," Jacquelyn said when her husband reached for more.

Edward put back the fries and took two onion rings instead, giving his wife a mischievous grin.

Jeffrey finished his burger and helped Edward polish off the mound of fries and rings. When the plate was empty, Edward leaned back, rubbed his stomach and let out a loud belch.

"Dad," Jeffrey exclaimed.

"What? It was a good meal." Edward patted his stomach.

"Have you ever burped before?"

"He's started doing it all the time," Jacquelyn said sourly.

"Since when?"

"Since I survived a heart attack. My perspective has changed, haven't you noticed?"

Jeffrey thought back on the months since his father's attack in August. Edward had returned to work by December, but Jeffrey now recalled his father being home on each of the few occasions he'd stopped by the house. If he'd known Edward was going to be there, Jeffrey probably wouldn't have visited, yet each time Edward had been more relaxed. The two men had always had Jacquelyn as a buffer between them, but Jeffrey realized they needed her less and less.

"Did you go into the office today?" Jeffrey asked.

"I stopped in for a couple of hours after I went to the junk yard and got pictures of your truck, but there wasn't anything pressing to attend to. Speaking of which..." Edward stood and moved to the kitchen counter. When he returned, he pushed a camera across the table to Jeffrey. "I think it's time you got a new truck."

Jeffrey turned the camera on and scrolled through the photos. The damage was worse than he'd expected. He turned off the camera. "It will definitely cost more to repair than the truck is worth."

Edward nodded. "That's what the guy at the junk yard said."

"I hate car shopping. That's part of the reason I hung onto the truck for so long."

"Tell me what you want and I'll take care of it," Edward offered.

"Thanks, but I can manage it." Jeffrey balled up his burger wrapper and napkin. "Maybe I can go shopping tomorrow."

"If you know what kind of vehicle you want, we can arrange for one to be delivered," Edward pressed.

In the years Jeffrey had spent away from his parents he'd forgotten about the way problems like getting a new car were instantly solved with a single phone call. The idea of having to visit dealerships gave him a headache and he had plenty in savings to pay for a new truck outright.

"A new Tacoma is fine, any color but red, and I don't want to pay more than twenty thousand," Jeffrey said.

"What kind of car can you get for twenty thousand?" Edward protested.

"The kind of car I want. I don't need anything fancy." He gritted his teeth, anticipating his father's next argument.

"All right, if that's what you want. I'll make a few calls." Edward stood and headed toward his office.

"It was nice of you to let him do that," Jacquelyn said.

Jeffrey shrugged. "It saves me the hassle."

"Is there anything in particular you would like to do this evening?"

Jeffrey scratched his head. "I've watched too much TV in the past couple of days. I need to do something else."

"You want to look in the library for a book?"

Jeffrey laughed. "I don't think there's anything in there I'd be interested in."

"Oh, I don't know. Your father has started reading thriller novels full of espionage, intrigue, and secret societies."

Jeffrey raised a questioning eyebrow. "Are you sure you brought the right man home from the hospital?"

"He still has his moments when he's a stubborn mule, but he's mellowed tremendously."

"You feel up for a game of Scrabble?"

Jacquelyn's face brightened. "I'll get the board. Where do you want to play?"

"In here is fine with me. We'll be closer to the snacks when the burger wears off."

"I can't believe you're already thinking about food again." Jacquelyn stood. "I'll be right back."

CHAPTER FIFTY THREE

Lizzie looked across the street as she got out of her car and saw Mae sitting on her front porch. She crossed and sat down in the rocking chair next to her.

"That's a sparkly new ring you have there," Mae said.

"Isn't it perfect?" Lizzie gushed, lifting her hand to inspect the ring for the hundredth time.

"I'm so happy for you. How did he propose?"

Lizzie giggled. "Oh, Mae, it was unbelievable." She told her friend the story of the weekend, how hopeless everything had seemed and how it had all changed in an instant.

Mae rocked back and forth, her hands clasped on her lap. "God does work in mysterious ways. It may be a cliché, but it is still true."

"I suppose you're right." Lizzie looked out over the neighborhood. Several houses down, two boys kicked a ball back and forth. Next to them, a man was out mowing his grass, probably too busy watching sports over the weekend to do it. A couple of women pushed strollers down the sidewalk from the park.

"Now, if Mr. Phillips wants to sell the house, you will have a place to go," Mae said, interrupting the quiet and jolting Lizzie from her reverie.

"Just because Ian and I are getting married doesn't mean I want to give up my house."

"Surely the two of you will want to find a place of your own."

"There's a lot we need to figure out," Lizzie said, realizing for the first time how much her life was about to change.

Mae stopped rocking and fixed Lizzie with a motherly stare. "You are part of a pair, things are not all about you anymore. You will both have to compromise on things."

Lizzie let the words sink in. She was part of a pair, she had been for months, but she hadn't acted like it. Had Mae recognized that already?

"You're right," Lizzie said. "I've been on my own for so long, sometimes I forget what it's like to be a part of something larger."

Mae started her rocker again. "You'll be fine as long as you remember that from now on."

"I guess I should call Mr. Phillips and make arrangements for him to come over." Lizzie returned home, taking the steps to her front porch two at a time. She pushed open the front door and gazed at the familiar living room and kitchen, remembering how dilapidated the house had been upon her first visit. When Mr. Phillips had visited last summer, she had been proud to show him all the improvements she had made. Now she feared those improvements would cause her to lose the first place she'd felt at home since her parents had died.

She heard a car door close behind her, but thought nothing of it. She stepped inside and pushed the door closed, failing to notice it didn't close completely. An arm snaked around her waist and her breath caught in her throat.

CHAPTER FIFTY FOUR

She tried to scream but nothing came out. Then she smelled pine and rain and her body relaxed. She twisted her head around and met Ian's lips.

"You scared me," she whispered.

"You should make sure to close your door," he murmured before kissing her again.

"If all burglars taste this good, I may leave the door open more often."

Ian released her and she turned to face him. He scowled, but she could see laughter in his eyes. She took his hand and led him to the sofa.

"What are you doing here?" she asked as they sat down.

"I missed you."

Lizzie rested her head on his shoulder. "I missed you too."

"Would you like to get some dinner?"

"Let's order in. I'm too comfortable to go out."

"Chinese?"

Lizzie nodded. Ian called in their order then slipped an arm around Lizzie and pulled her closer.

"Any luck finding a way to reach Ron and Emma?" he asked.

"I called the group they are sponsored by. They gave me the name of a business they work with in the town closest to the village Ron and Emma are serving. The business can get express mail and often makes deliveries to the village, so the letter could be delivered in less than a week."

"That's great news."

"Have you thought about when we should get married?" Lizzie lifted her head and looked at Ian.

"I'm at your disposal. Whenever you say, I'll be there."

"Be serious. I can't make this decision on my own."

"I am serious. I'm in between clients right now so I can plan my schedule around the wedding."

"What about your parents? They can't drop everything to accommodate us."

"Ron and Emma won't be home until August, so it's not like we're getting married next week. There's plenty of time for them to arrange their schedules."

"Sometime in the fall might be nice." Lizzie reached for a magazine on the coffee table.

"You already stocked up on bridal magazines?" Ian teased.

"This is an old one we had at work." Lizzie flipped through the pages, not looking for anything in particular.

"Tell me about the wedding you dreamed of as a little girl." Ian ran his hand through her hair then massaged the back of her neck. She lowered her head, enjoying the feel of his fingers on her tense muscles.

"I never dreamed about my wedding, only the reception. Publix used to have these giant wedding cakes on display, three tiers with stairways to smaller cakes on either side. I admired them every time mom took me shopping with her. I envisioned a cake like that and lots of dancing." Lizzie laughed at the memory.

"Big cake and dancing. That we can do." Ian took the magazine. "What about the dress? Surely you pictured yourself in a gorgeous dress."

Lizzie leaned back on the couch, propped her heels on the coffee table and wrapped her arms around her knees. "I had a dream once that I was walking down an aisle in a black gown, a southern belle style gown, and my bridesmaids wore midnight blue. It was a strange dream and I woke up feeling...strange."

Ian shifted and turned his body toward her. "You really haven't been planning a wedding your whole life have you?"

"Is that so odd?"

"I don't know. I guess I've always been under the impression that every girl has her wedding planned before she graduates high school." He tossed the magazine onto the table. "This girl I dated in high school had our whole lives planned out after we'd been dating three weeks. She showed me a binder she'd made for her wedding with photos of dresses, flowers, even the favors she planned to give out. It was creepy."

Lizzie gazed at Ian, trying to picture him as a teenager. "Was she devastated when you broke up with her?"

"What makes you so sure I broke up with her?"

Lizzie touched his cheek. "What girl is crazy enough to dump you?"

Ian kissed her finger as it slid past his mouth. "Be careful, you might inflate my ego."

The doorbell rang and Lizzie laughed. "Dinner's here."

She unfolded her legs to stand, but Ian was already off the couch, headed for the door. He paid the deliveryman and accepted a plastic bag in return.

"Thanks, you have a good night," he said as he shut the door.

Lizzie went to the kitchen for plates and silverware. "What do you want to drink?"

"Water is fine." Ian pulled containers from the bag and set them on the dining room table. Lizzie joined him, carrying two bottles of water, plates, and forks.

Ian said a blessing and they dished out food from each container. Lizzie smiled to herself at how comfortable they were together, how easily they passed the food, without having to say a word.

"I brought something I want you to look at after we eat," Ian said.

"What is it?"

Ian shoveled a forkful of rice into his mouth and chewed, then reached for his water. "Sheila said I should put more residential plans on the website for clients to view."

"But you don't want to build houses that are all the same."

Ian pointed at her, his eyes bright. "I knew you'd understand and that's what I told her, but she made a good point about using them as a starting point. I drew several different plans over the weekend. I'm pretty sure that's what gave Sheila the idea."

"That's what you were doing when I was calling you?" Lizzie pursed her lips.

"I work when I'm upset."

"Does that apply to a honey-do-list as well or just sketching?"

Ian set down his fork and studied the ceiling for a minute. "I don't know. I've never had a honey-do-list. Did you have something in mind?"

Lizzie batted her eyes. "Not yet, but I'm sure I can come up with some things for you to take care of in the future."

They finished their meal and cleaned up the leftovers, chatting about the events of the day.

"How long will Tammy have to stay in Texas?" Ian asked as they settled back on the couch.

"I don't know. We've mentioned to the general manager several times that we need a second convention manager. Even if we had a part-time person it would be a tremendous help. Maybe now I can convince him to hire someone."

"Maybe we should put off trying to plan the wedding until Tammy returns. I don't want you overextending yourself."

"I know she has a ton of vacation time since she can never take more than a day or two off, but I can't imagine she'll be gone more than a month."

"Maybe we don't lock in a date until we know when she will be back at work."

Lizzie sighed. "Venues book up months, even years in advance, but since we don't have any particular location in mind, I guess a few more weeks won't hurt."

"You can start looking at dresses and flowers and all those other things."

"Don't you mean we can start looking?" She tapped his chest.

He chuckled. "Of course. Whatever you want me to look at I will happily agree to."

"Wasn't there something you wanted to show me?"

Ian started to get up from the couch, but sat back down and slipped an arm around Lizzie's shoulders. "It can wait. Let's talk more about the wedding."

CHAPTER FIFTY FIVE

Jeffrey cracked open one eye and looked around the room. It hadn't been a dream; he was in his old bedroom at his parents' house. He tried to roll his shoulder; maybe a tiny bit more motion. The pain seemed less, too. He sat up, careful not to put any weight on his injured arm.

A duffel bag sat on a chair in the corner with clothes Jacquelyn had collected from his house the previous night. He reached in and pulled out a fresh pair of jeans and a t-shirt. He crossed the hallway to the bathroom, where fresh towels had been laid out on the marble countertop along with a selection of toiletries.

Washing with one arm was difficult, but he was starting to get the hang of it. His shower still took twice as long as before the accident, but the heat felt good on his battered body.

"Good morning," Jacquelyn greeted as he entered the kitchen. She sat at the breakfast bar with a cup of coffee and a magazine.

"Morning," Jeffrey replied. A pair of coffee cups sat next to the pot and he filled one, adding half a teaspoon of sugar.

"How are you feeling?" Jacquelyn asked.

"A little better."

"What are your plans for today?"

"I need to go over some paperwork, check in with Jenny to see how things are going on the site, and have the bank send a check for the new truck."

"Are you happy with what your father found for you?"

As much as he hated to admit it, Edward had found exactly what Jeffrey would have chosen himself. "It must have killed him to get a base model."

"It's good experience for him, in the event we lose all our money he will know what to expect."

"You're not in any trouble, are you?" Jeffrey sat down and took a banana from a fruit bowl in the center of the table.

"Not that I know of." Jacquelyn slid off the bar chair and went to the coffee pot to refill her mug. "Do you want to use your father's office? He should be gone most of the day."

"If the weather's nice, I think I'll go out on the patio."

"It should be a beautiful day. I can have the housekeeper set up a table for you."

Throbbing in his shoulder reminded him of his limitations, stopping any protest he may have made. He finished the banana and coffee. "Maybe she can bring a pitcher of water out as well. I have to take these ibuprofen every four hours to keep the pain manageable."

Jacquelyn nodded and Jeffrey went in search of his briefcase. He found it in the living room, by the couch where he'd left it the previous morning.

"I can get that for you."

Jeffrey turned to find Helen, the housekeeper, hurrying into the room. "Helen, it's good to see you."

"It's nice to have you home, Mr. Jeffrey." Helen bent over and collected the briefcase.

"Why haven't I seen you on my previous visits?" Jeffrey asked.

"You know the help isn't to be seen," Helen said with a wink.

Jeffrey rolled his eyes. "How's your family?"

"They are well. My daughter Mina got married two months ago." Helen's face beamed with pride.

"Congratulations. I'm sure she was a beautiful bride." Jeffrey tried to remember the last time he'd seen Mina. It must have been before he went to college. She was only a year younger than him and they'd often played together as children. Her long dark hair and big round eyes had bewitched him as a teenager.

Helen set the briefcase on the patio table. "I'll bring you some of my special water. I infuse it with slices of lemon and sprigs of rosemary. I think some cheese and crackers would be good too since you'll be taking ibuprofen."

"You are too good for us, Helen." Jeffrey kissed her flushed cheek.

Once he was alone, Jeffrey looked around the patio and found a wicker chair with a thick cushion. He dragged it closer to the table, picked up the laptop and settled down to work.

CHAPTER FIFTY SIX

Waiters and housekeepers hurried along the service corridor, passing Lizzie as she made her way to Tammy's office.

"How was the meeting?" Tammy asked.

"Don't get me started," Lizzie groaned. The morning had been eaten away by an impromptu meeting of the front desk managers to announce the merger with Ryland Resorts.

"That good."

"Nothing new on how the merger may affect us. I don't think it will at our level, but I'm sure there will be duplications on the corporate level that will have to be addressed."

"Maybe there's someone in corporate who'd like to come help me out," Tammy said with a hopeful smile.

"That would be a blessing for everyone. How's your mom doing?"

"The doctor said she's doing well. I found a flight leaving tomorrow morning, but I don't know how long I'll need to stay out there."

"That's what I was afraid of." Lizzie sank back in her chair and touched the ring.

"I know, I hate to be such an imposition." Tammy frowned. "As soon as she can travel I can bring her back here."

"No, it's not that," Lizzie said. "You take as much time as you need to care for your mom, that's more important than anything."

"You already have so much work, though."

Lizzie waved her hand dismissively.

"Wait, what was that?" Tammy stood and came around the desk. She grabbed Lizzie's hand and squealed with delight. "Why didn't you tell me you were engaged?"

"It happened over the weekend." Lizzie felt her face flush as she looked at the ring. "When you told me about your mom last night, I forgot about everything else."

"Have you talked about a date?"

"We talked about it last night and agreed not to lock anything in until we know more about your situation."

I'm just causing you problems on all sides." Tammy leaned back on the desk, wringing her hands.

"You didn't make your mom fall. God has a reason for these things happening at the same time. Everything will work out just as He has planned it."

"I don't know how you can be so calm." Tammy sniffled and reached for a tissue.

"I put on a wedding during a hurricane with only emergency power. How's a little corporate merger and double-duty workload going to stop me?"

Tammy tried to laugh, but it came out as a choked sob. Lizzie stood and pulled her friend into a comforting embrace. "Why don't you catch me up on the calendar and then go home? Take some time to rest before you pack."

Tammy returned to her chair and handed Lizzie a binder. Lizzie opened it and found a table of contents before several tabbed sections. She smiled at how similar she and Tammy were. Organization was a way of life for them.

"The banquet event orders are done for the first five groups." Tammy reviewed all of the events scheduled through the end of May and Lizzie followed along in the binder, making notes when needed.

"This doesn't seem too bad," Lizzie said an hour later when they finished. "Forward your phone to me and go home. I'll let everyone know I'm covering for you."

"I want to send out some emails to let the clients know you're taking over for a while then I'll head out."

Lizzie stood, tucking the binder under her arm. "Have a safe trip."

CHAPTER FIFTY SEVEN

"Here they are now." A broad shouldered man with slick black hair and hazel eyes rose from the table as Lizzie and Stephen approached.

"Sorry we're late, James." Lizzie leaned into the man's hug and kissed him on the cheek. "I was lost in a convention file when Stephen told me it was time to leave."

"I heard about Tammy's mom. How's she doing?" Stephanie, a petite brunette sitting across the table asked. Stephanie was the nurturing one of the group, always on top of get well cards and organizing celebrations for special occasions.

"Tammy has a flight to Texas in the morning. The doctor said her mom is doing well, but I'm sure Tammy will be happy to see for herself."

The natural group leader, James asked, "Who is covering for her while she's out?"

"That would be me." Lizzie gave a wry grin and moved around the table to take the seat next to Stephanie. Stephen sat down next to James and greetings were exchanged with the other Concierge Club members around the table.

Lizzie felt a kick under the table and glanced toward Stephen. He waggled his eyebrows and nodded, then reached for his glass and knife. The tinny ring of metal against glass quieted the table. All eyes turned to Stephen, who gazed intently at Lizzie.

"I guess Stephen would like for me to share some news with you." Lizzie looked at the expectant faces of her many friends, realizing for the first time how much these people meant to her. Her gaze rested on James and she remembered their conversation almost a year ago, when she thought she'd never find love. His eyes met hers and she smiled. "Ian and I are getting married."

Squeals and cheers filled the air, chairs scrapping against the floor, bodies moving, everyone trying to get up at the same time. Lizzie felt hands on her shoulders and pushed her own chair back, standing to accept hugs and extending her hand for all of the women to admire the ring.

After everyone had settled back into their places, someone called from the end of the table, "How did he propose?"

Lizzie felt her face redden. "I didn't make it easy," she said before sharing an abbreviated version of the weekend's events.

"He proposed in church?" Mona snorted with laughter.

"He's been carrying the ring around for two months?" James asked, then nodded. "Good man. I like a man who's prepared."

Lizzie giggled and several others added their own chuckles.

"When's the wedding?" Patricia asked.

"We've only been engaged a couple of days." Lizzie feigned exasperation.

"I know a fabulous baker," Stephanie said. "Her cakes are to die for."

"Thanks, Steph. We'll have to compare notes. I know a couple of pretty amazing pastry chefs, too."

Talking about the wedding made it seem more real. The big decisions, like place and time, started to seem like the easy part. Choosing who her bridesmaids would be now became the daunting question. She'd never been a girly girl and most of her close friends were men. Now she listened as the married women shared stories of planning their own weddings and the last two single ladies, Stephanie and Mona, interjected with their own dreams.

"You're awfully quiet," Stephanie whispered.

Lizzie shrugged. "Thinking about planning a wedding; I've helped Tammy on at least a dozen at the hotel, but doing it for myself is a different thing altogether, isn't it?"

Stephanie reached over and squeezed Lizzie's hand. "You have all of us to help out. At this table you have access to more resources than most wedding planners. Your wedding is going to be perfect."

Lizzie nodded and swallowed the lump forming in her throat. Maybe she had better girl friends than she knew.

The conversation lulled when a server appeared to take their orders. James stood and lifted his water glass. "I propose a toast. To Lizzie, may many years of happiness lie ahead of you."

Glasses clinked and another round of congratulations were expressed. Lizzie dabbed at her eyes with her napkin. "Enough about me. What is everyone doing for Bacchus Bash?"

Patricia spoke up first. "Our chef is going to be serving bananas foster."

CHAPTER FIFTY EIGHT

By Friday, Jeffrey was ready to return to his own house. Reports from Jenny at the office had been so positive he'd had the confidence to take the whole week off for his bones to mend.

Helen had spoiled him as he enjoyed the sunshine and fresh air on the patio in the mornings and worked in the library in the afternoons. She seemed capable of hearing his stomach growl from anywhere in the house and would appear moments later carrying a tray of food. He was certain he'd gained ten pounds during his stay.

"Are you sure you're going to be okay on your own?" Jacquelyn asked as she carried his duffel bag to the new truck.

"I'll be fine. I can't stay here until my bones are completely healed, that'll take weeks, but I do feel much stronger now." Jeffrey kissed his mother on the cheek.

Jacquelyn opened the passenger door and set the duffel bag on the seat. "You'll call if you need anything, won't you?"

"Yes, mother." Jeffrey sighed.

He climbed into the truck and took a minute to get acquainted with the new dashboard. He was once again grateful it was his left arm that was out of commission, making driving less of a chore. He'd allowed Edward to secure an automatic transmission rather than the manual he preferred, since it would be easier to handle in his current condition.

"Drive safely," Jacquelyn called as he backed down the driveway.

It felt good to be out again, moving along the highway. He enjoyed getting to know the new truck, listening to the sound of the engine, identifying rattles as he bumped along the worn pavement. He arrived at the bungalow, eager to be home.

There was a foul odor when he opened the front door. Dropping the duffel bag on the couch, he moved through the living room, into the kitchen where the smell grew stronger. A full garbage bag sat next to the sink; he'd forgotten to carry it outside before leaving Monday morning.

"Where's Helen when I need her?" he mumbled.

With the trash taken to the outside bin, he found a can of air freshener and fogged the room with freshness.

The phone rang and he groaned. She's calling already, he thought to himself.

"I'm fine, mom," he answered.

"Good to know, but it's Michelle."

Jeffrey sat up straighter, shaking off his tiredness. "Hey, how are you?"

"I'm all right. You sound tired. We can talk another time."

"No, I had to take the garbage out. It's harder to do one handed than you might think."

"I bet."

Several seconds passed and Michelle didn't say anything more. Jeffrey twisted on the couch, so his feet were propped up on one end, his head pressed against the other. "How's the new song coming?" he asked.

"There isn't any new song," Michelle admitted. "I only said that so I could leave."

"I kind of figured."

"Why didn't you say anything?"

"It was obvious you were uncomfortable, for whatever reason. I wasn't going to make it worse."

"You aren't even mad at me, are you?"

Jeffrey could hear the surprise in her words and tried to imagine how she looked as she said them. He thought she might be rubbing the scar above her right eye. He wondered how she'd gotten it, but knew the story must involve a man. He remembered she seemed to touch it each time she was uneasy around him.

"No, I'm not mad. Confused, worried, yeah, but not mad."

"Can I make it up to you?"

"What did you have in mind?"

"Dinner? I could cook for you, but I wouldn't recommend that, or I can bring some take out."

"Take out is fine. My kitchen isn't stocked with many cooking utensils and I don't think I can handle driving again this evening."

"There's an Outback between my place and yours. I can pick something up there."

"Mmm, a steak sounds really good." Jeffrey gave her his order and ended the call. He looked around the living room. It was just as clean as the last time she'd been over, which wasn't saying much after the days he'd spent with his parents. The bungalow had a lived in look he couldn't imagine ever existing at their house. He closed his eyes and waited for Michelle to arrive.

CHAPTER FIFTY NINE

Lizzie stepped out of her car and closed her eyes. She drew in a deep breath, inhaling the colors of red, pink, purple, and white. She opened her eyes and feasted on the profusion of blooms. The buds on the trimmed rose bushes along the front porch seemed fuller than yesterday. At the corner of the porch, a short hibiscus tree sported five new pink blooms, and in the neighbor's yard, a fat magnolia tree wore dozens of large, white blossoms. Spring was bursting forth all around her.

Oh, how I'd love to get married in the spring, she thought. She stepped off the walkway onto the cushy grass and moved closer to one of the rose bushes. She leaned close to one of the half opened buds and sniffed it. It was sweet and fresh.

"Stopping to smell the roses?"

Lizzie straightened and turned to see Mae on the sidewalk. "Isn't it a beautiful evening?"

"That it is." Mae strolled up the driveway and met Lizzie at the front porch steps. "You're in a good mood."

"Why shouldn't I be? The most wonderful man in the world wants to marry me." Lizzie opened the front door and Mae followed her inside. "Of course I have no idea when we'll actually be able to get married."

"There can't be trouble already." Mae's brow knitted in concern.

"Nothing a little patience won't overcome." Lizzie removed a pitcher of iced tea from the refrigerator and poured two tall glasses.

"That's a good attitude to have." Mae gave an approving nod.

"Mae, where did you get married?" The women took seats around the dining room table and Lizzie set her glass down.

Mae's pale blue eyes softened. "Lewis and I had our wedding in a beautiful garden in Virginia. So many flowers were blooming I felt like I was in a fairytale world. My bouquet had a dozen different blooms."

Mae chuckled. "There were bees everywhere. When we were saying our vows, Lewis kept swatting at one that was determined to get under my veil."

Lizzie giggled at the image. "I was thinking how nice it would be to get married in the spring with flowers all around, but maybe that's not such a good idea after all. Besides, I can't imagine waiting another year."

"What happened to your patience?" Mae quipped.

"I know, but a fall wedding could be nice too. Especially if we had it in Connecticut, with the changing leaves."

"Are you thinking of having it there? Is that were Ian's family is?"

"We haven't really talked about it yet. It seems right, though, since he has more family than I do."

"Family isn't only blood," Mae said. "You've built a nice family around you here. I've seen all the people who helped you get this place into shape, and everyone who came to your housewarming party. Don't you think they'd like to see you married?"

Lizzie ran her finger around the rim of her glass. "I didn't think about that."

Mae took a long sip of her tea. "When is Mr. Phillips coming by?"

"Any minute now." Lizzie felt her body tense at the thought.

"Whatever happens with him, remember you are going to be fine." Mae finished her tea and stood. "I better get home. Avery is taking me out to dinner tonight."

"Thanks for coming by." Lizzie walked Mae to the front door and waited for her to cross the street safely before closing the door.

CHAPTER SIXTY

Michelle touched up her make-up, taking extra care to cover the small scar over her eye. She ran a brush through her thick, wavy hair, then a lint brush over her shirt to remove the strands that fell with each stroke. "I shed like a cat," she mumbled.

Her order from Outback would be ready for pick up in thirty minutes. She paced the apartment, collecting papers scattered around the rooms and sorting them into piles.

She picked up the phone to call Wendy, then put it down. Wendy already believed Michelle had feelings for Jeffrey. She didn't have feelings for him, she just felt bad for the way she'd acted. It had been immature.

Ten minutes passed and she couldn't wait any longer. She left the apartment, slamming the door behind her. She reached the restaurant and pulled into one of the parking spots reserved for takeout. A hostess came outside before Michelle had even turned off her engine.

"What's the name on the order?" the hostess asked.

"Burton, Michelle."

"Let me check." The hostess went inside and was gone for several minutes before returning with a large paper bag.

"Here you go, Ms. Burton. Have a nice night."

"Thank you." Michelle took the bag and set it on the floor of the passenger seat.

A new truck was parked in Jeffrey's driveway when Michelle arrived. She wondered if it was a rental or if he'd already gotten an insurance check to replace his wrecked one. She collected the bag of food and made her way to the front door where she knocked and waited, her heart quickening when she heard movement inside.

Jeffrey opened the door. "The food smells great."

Michelle entered, unsure where to go. "Do you want to eat at the coffee table?"

"No, I have a real table. It's small, but it works."

She followed him into the kitchen. A bistro-style table was tucked into a corner, already set with plates, silverware, and glasses of iced tea. She set the bag on the stove and pulled out the containers, opening the first lid to see which meal was inside.

"This one is yours. Do you want me to put it on the plate for you?"

"If you wouldn't mind. I'd hate to drop it on the floor."

She placed the large steak on the plate and sliced it into manageable pieces before adding the baked potato, and setting small containers of butter and sour cream on the side. She opened the second container and removed a filet mignon and baked potato, careful not to spill any of the juice from the box. Two loaves of bread wrapped in aluminum foil came next, and were set in the middle of the table.

"You got extra bread." Jeffrey smiled. "I love their bread."

"Me too. We can each have our own loaf."

Jeffrey pulled out a chair and motioned for Michelle to be seated. She hesitated, checking to make sure everything they needed was on the table. Finding nothing missing, she sat. Jeffrey helped her scoot closer to the table before being seated himself.

"Do you mind if I say a blessing over the food?" he asked. When she shook her head he reached for her hand.

"Dear Lord, thank you for this food. Allow it to bring nourishment to our bodies. Thank you for Michelle and her kind hearted generosity in bringing me this meal. In your precious name I pray, Amen."

Michelle hadn't closed her eyes during the prayer, instead she watched Jeffrey. His face grew peaceful as he spoke each word and she felt a tender tug on her heart.

Jeffrey gave her hand a tiny squeeze before he let go. "Let's eat."

Michelle cut into her filet and took several bites; the meat was so tender it melted in her mouth as she savored the flame-grilled flavor.

"This is really good," Jeffrey said when he was halfway through his steak.

"I didn't think to get any dessert."

"That's okay. I don't think I would have room for it." Jeffrey finished his baked potato and tore off a hunk of bread from his loaf.

"Why aren't you mad at me?" Michelle asked.

Jeffrey set down the knife he'd been using to butter the bread and met her gaze. "There's nothing for me to be mad about. You didn't want to be here in the first place. I appreciated that you came, but I wasn't going to force you to stay. I want us to be friends."

"What if I want to be more than friends?" Michelle couldn't believe she'd said that. "Wait, I didn't..." She could feel the color rising to her cheeks and looked toward the door.

Jeffrey touched her hand. "You don't have to run away."

"I didn't mean that." Michelle touched her forehead.

"I like you, a lot, but I don't think either of us is ready for a relationship. I'm still getting comfortable being alone, finding my way through my faith. You, I don't know what your baggage is, and I don't need to, but until you have faced that," Jeffrey paused and reached across the table to touch her scar. She flinched, surprised he'd noticed it, and he took his hand away.

"Until you can see me without thinking of whatever that scar represents, you won't trust me completely."

CHAPTER SIXTY ONE

Lizzie heard the sound of an engine outside. She moved to the window and saw a black Lincoln Town car pulling to a stop on the street. Mr. Phillips had arrived.

She pasted on her most charming smile and opened the front door. The doors of the car opened and a man dressed in an expensive-looking suit appeared followed by an attractive woman with dark hair and fair skin.

Jacob Phillips strode up the driveway, his smile displaying perfect teeth."Ms. Reynolds, it's good to see you. I'd like you to meet my wife, Melinda."

Lizzie froze at the sight of the woman's eyes and beak-like nose. They were identical to those of her son, Ralph Anderson, the man who had stalked and attacked Lizzie shortly after she'd renovated the house.

The woman extended her hand, but Lizzie couldn't move to accept it. She felt the old fear constricting her throat.

"Ms. Reynolds, are you all right?" Jacob touched her arm and she flinched.

Melinda retracted her hand and frowned. "I'm sorry. I forget how much Ralph and I look alike."

Lizzie swallowed the taste of bile that threatened to spew from her clenched lips. "Forgive me, Mrs. Phillips. Your eyes, just..."

"Not at all, dear. I understand Ralph caused you a great deal of trouble, for which I am profoundly disappointed in him."

Lizzie nodded. "Come inside."

She stepped aside, allowing Jacob and Melinda to look around. She tried to see the home through their eyes and felt self-conscious about her decorating style.

"This is charming," Melinda gushed. "You've made good use of such a small space."

"Do you want me to show you around or would you prefer to look on your own?"

"Please do," Jacob said. "I'd like to hear about the things you've added to the place."

She'd hoped they would want to view the house on their own. "I had the floors repaired due to warping, particularly near the broken windows where rain had blown in multiple times. Then there was the hurricane that put a hole in the roof and flooded the house so the floors were torn up again."

Lizzie walked them down the hall to the bedrooms. "Friends pitched in with painting and I had a granite overlay made for the kitchen counters. The claw-foot bathtub was a challenge, but I scrubbed it until it shined again."

When they returned from the bedrooms, Lizzie noticed Jacob stop in front of three picture frames.

"You kept them," he said with a sad smile.

"They are part of the house. I had new copies made shortly after I gave you the originals." Lizzie stood beside him, gazing at the photos of three trees drawn onto a wall.

"Do you remember where the drawings were?" Melinda asked.

Lizzie pointed at a wall to the right of the front door. "I hated painting over them, but I will always know they are there."

Jacob moved to the wall. "Can you show me where, exactly?"

Lizzie joined him and placed her hand on the wall at the height of her waist. "This was the tallest tree."

Jacob placed his hand next to hers. She gave him a moment before stepping to the right a few feet. "This was the second tallest."

Again Jacob touched the wall, this time getting down on his knees so where the top of tree would have been was level with his eyes. Lizzie looked away to give him privacy.

"Where was the first one?" His voice quavered and Lizzie's heart went out to him.

She moved to the other side of the window and got down on her knees, touching a spot no more than two feet off the ground. Jacob knelt beside her and she reached out for his hand. She gently placed it on the wall.

Melinda came up behind them and placed her hands on Jacob's shoulders. Lizzie looked up at the woman and saw the love Melinda had for her husband. Lizzie scooted away from the couple and stood up, her knees popping as she did so, but the couple remained undisturbed.

Lizzie went to the kitchen and worked with silent efficiency to pour three glasses of wine. She knew it was probably far below the quality her guests were accustomed to, but she felt the occasion warranted a toast. A full five minutes passed before Jacob moved. Melinda helped him to his feet. Lizzie caught sight of him tucking a handkerchief into his pocket before he turned to face her.

"Thank you for putting so much love into restoring this house," Jacob said, his voice rough with emotion.

Lizzie offered the wine, which they both accepted. Melinda held her glass high. "A toast to the past, may it live in our memories forever, and to the future, may it be filled with love and friendship."

They clinked glasses and took a long drink. "Ms. Reynolds, this house is yours for as long as you want it. I've been thinking about you a lot since we last met. I wasn't around much the final months of my mother's life. I didn't even know about this house until her will was read a couple of years ago. Even then I couldn't be bothered to do anything about it.

"When you gave me the photos of her drawings, I started thinking about how self-involved I was and how I had missed out on experiences because they would have required me to give up my time. I could have been the one to discover those drawings if I'd taken the time to come down here to deal with the house."

Melinda placed a hand on her husband's arm. "He spends more time at home now, and I have you to thank for that."

"All I did was restore an abandoned house because I was searching for a place to call home." Lizzie fought back tears that threatened to choke her when she compared how the loss of her own parents and the death of Jacob's mother had unexpectedly brought them together.

"The process of renovation opened my eyes to the people who care about me and reminded me that a house becomes a home when it is filled with love and dreams."

Melinda sniffled, Jacob cleared his throat, and Lizzie blinked back the water filling her eyes, then as if in agreement, they all laughed.

"Look at us, a bunch of blubbering fools," Jacob croaked.

Lizzie went to get a box of tissues from an end table and passed the box around.

"Thank you for bringing me here, Jacob." Melinda leaned into her husband and he slipped his arm around her.

"You are welcome here anytime," Lizzie said. "Who would like more wine?"

CHAPTER SIXTY TWO

A whippoorwill called through the quiet evening. Lizzie stood on the front porch, waving to Melinda and Jacob until they turned at the end of the street. She rested against one of the porch support columns, listening to the bird's call and enjoying the cool air on her skin. She scarcely knew Jacob and Melinda Phillips but after the intimate experience they had shared, now felt connected to them.

Her fears about Jacob's visit had been unfounded. Another example of the walls she built around herself that limited vulnerability and trust.

She looked across the street and saw Mae's door open. Her son Avery stepped out followed by his wife, Amy, and his brother, Liam. Laughter floated on the breeze. The family exchanged hugs before bouncing down the steps to their cars on the street. Lizzie waved when they looked in her direction. She waited until they were gone, then crossed the street and joined Mae in their customary rocking chairs.

"How was your visit with Mr. Phillips?" Mae asked.

"What a difference a week makes." Lizzie sighed. "Saturday, I was certain I was losing everything. Tonight, I realize I have more than I ever could have imagined."

"I take it he doesn't want you to move out then?"

"No, he told me I could stay as long as I like. His wife is a jewel. I can't imagine how Ralph turned out so horrible."

"Children are always the losers in divorce. Sometimes they are so filled with anger, no earthly love can overcome it."

"But God's love can. I'm going to start praying for Ralph. I could see Melinda is grieved by the way her son has turned out."

"Your prayers are the best thing you can give to that family."

"I've also been thinking about the wedding. You're right, I do have a lot of people here who would like to be part of it, but they couldn't afford to go to Connecticut. Ian's family can easily make the trip here, so I'm going to talk to him about having the wedding in Florida."

Mae smiled, delight dancing in her eyes. "I'm so happy to hear that. Are you any closer to setting a date?"

"I have a couple of ideas, but I have to run them by Ian first."

Mae nodded and turned her gaze back out onto the neighborhood. Lizzie thought of all the times before that she and Mae had kept watch over their neighbors like this. The same lights shone behind half-pulled curtains, the same dogs barked when a car passed by, the same strains of Bach played through an open window. All of this was home.

CHAPTER SIXTY THREE

Ian pulled to a stop in front of Lizzie's house. The front door opened before he'd stepped out of the car. She ran to him, her sundress flowing around her in a pink mist. He met her on the sidewalk and they shared a tender kiss that made his heart race.

"Your chariot, my lady." He bowed as he opened the car door for her.

"Are you sure Jeffrey can meet us at the restaurant?" she asked when Ian was seated and had started the car.

"He said the pain in his shoulder is easing off a little each day. Plus he doesn't have to drive far."

"I can't wait to tell him the news." Lizzie tapped her feet on the floorboard in, what Ian guessed, was a modified happy dance.

Ian wasn't so sure about how the meeting would go. Lizzie could spend time with just about any other man and Ian wouldn't feel jealous, but he couldn't deny the green monster that rose within him when he knew she was with Jeffrey.

He used the mid-morning traffic as an excuse not to respond, focusing on a car ahead of them that seemed lost. It would slow down, put on its turn signal, then speed up. Finally it turned, without signaling or slowing down. Ian relaxed his grip on the steering wheel.

"Why didn't you pass him?" Lizzie asked.

"I was afraid he'd change lanes when I tried." Ian shook his head. "He had no idea where he was going."

"Should I take the ring off until we tell him?"

Ian glanced over at Lizzie. Her brow creased with concern as she looked at the ring on her finger. "Why don't I hold that hand when we meet him and you can keep it under the table until we tell him, if that will make you more comfortable."

The crease disappeared and she placed her hand on his. Her skin was warm and soft, and the band of the ring against his knuckle felt solid and comforting. He down shifted to make the turn into the parking lot.

A hedge of roses in full bloom lined the walkway in front of the restaurant. Ian and Lizzie walked hand-in-hand beside it to the front door.

"Don't they smell wonderful?"

Ian leaned down and buried his nose in her hair. "Not as wonderful as you."

Lizzie bent forward, laughing. "Stop it, people will see."

"See what? Me with the most beautiful girl in the world? Let them see."

Inside the restaurant, they found Jeffrey waiting for them. Ian noticed the bruising on his face had faded and, aside from the cast and sling, he looked like his old self. No, not quite like his old self, Ian thought. There was something different.

Jeffrey's face brightened when he saw them and he stepped forward to give them each a hug. "Careful, not so tight," he said when Lizzie squeezed him.

"Sorry, sorry, did I hurt you?" Lizzie stepped back, her eyes wide in horror.

"It's okay. I'm already broken," Jeffrey joked.

"Are you sure?"

"I'm fine." Jeffrey patted her shoulder. "I think our table is ready."

They followed a hostess to a table near a window. Ian held out a chair for Lizzie and both men waited for her to be seated before sitting themselves.

"If I knew everyone would want to feed me after I broke my arm, I would have started breaking bones a long time ago." Jeffrey picked up his menu and Ian glanced at Lizzie. She gave him a small shake of her head.

The server came and took their orders. When they were alone again, Lizzie reached for Ian's hand under the table.

"We have some news to share," Ian said.

Jeffrey grinned. "Did you finally pop the question?"

Lizzie nodded, bursting with excitement, and brought her hand onto the table. "And I said yes."

Ian's mind tried to catch up. He watched Jeffrey examine the ring on Lizzie's finger and could see his lips moving but didn't hear the words. Lizzie nudged him and Ian turned his gaze to her.

"He asked what took you so long?" she said. Sunlight flashed in her eyes and he had to laugh.

"Does it matter? We're engaged now." He put his arm around Lizzie's shoulders.

"I'm happy for you two. I couldn't imagine either of you without the other."

Jeffrey's heartfelt congratulations surprised Ian. Something was different about him. He seemed to have shed the brooding that had clouded his face, even after giving his life to Christ.

"What's going on with you?" Ian asked.

Jeffrey dismissed the question. "Nothing as exciting as your news."

"I think it may be," Ian pressed. He saw the questioning look Lizzie gave him, but maintained eye contact with Jeffrey.

CHAPTER SIXTY FOUR

"I think Michelle may be close to accepting the Lord," Jeffrey said, his grin widening.

"That's wonderful!" Lizzie exclaimed. "What happened?"

Jeffrey told them of Michelle's visits the past week and their conversation over dinner the previous night. He looked to Lizzie. "You know she and I have been talking about faith off and on since February."

Lizzie nodded. "You said she seemed open to discussion, but you weren't pressing."

"I've been trying to lead her by example, to show her love like Jesus showed those around him. It's been hard. There have been times when I wanted to shake her and make her see how much she's missing." Jeffrey grimaced. "I guess you both felt that way about me at times."

Ian felt his heart soften toward Jeffrey, remembering the time in college when they had been close friends. He thought about Camylle. "She would be so proud of you right now," Ian whispered.

"Do you think so?" Jeffrey's eyes watered and Ian tried to choke back the lump rising in his throat.

Ian nodded, unable to speak. He felt Lizzie twine her fingers with his and noticed her doing the same across the table with Jeffrey.

"Last night, when Michelle and I talked about relationships, I explained how I'm working to build my relationship with God, and I could see she was finally getting it. That it's just like building a relationship between two people. Her walls are starting to come down." The tears left Jeffrey's voice, replaced by excitement.

"She might even go to church with me tomorrow."

"I'm so happy for you," Lizzie said.

"I know there's still a long way to go, but it's a start. She's so different from Camylle, but I can be myself around her. My new self. I'm pretty sure she likes the new me better than the old me anyway." Jeffrey chortled. "I was a real jerk before."

"Not all the time," Lizzie assured him. "I'm continually astounded at the people God brings into our lives and the long reaching effects they can have."

Ian looked around the table and couldn't agree more. If he and Jeffrey hadn't run into each other that night in August, he may never have met Lizzie. If Lizzie had taken cookies to any other construction site seeking help with her renovations, Jeffrey may never have come to know the Lord. How far beyond the circle of this table did their lives reach?

CHAPTER SIXTY FIVE

News of Lizzie's engagement spread throughout Hotel Lago. Every day someone new congratulated her on the upcoming wedding. Stephen watched his mentor accept their congratulations with a blush. He'd known she was popular with the staff, but this outpouring of support brought home to him how important she was to the hotel. What would happen if she left one day?

"Good morning." Lizzie breezed into the office, her sing-song greeting pulling Stephen from his reverie.

"You're in a good mood," he said.

"I should be exhausted, with all the groups we've had coming in, but I'm finally going to have some time to work on wedding plans tonight." Lizzie set her purse on Stephen's desk and gave him a look that made him feel like he was a movie star. "You've been a tremendous help around here."

She reached into her purse and pulled out a small box. "I wanted to give you a little something."

"You didn't have to do that," Stephen protested. "I've only been doing my job."

Lizzie shook her head. "You've kept on top of things, made sure our guests are receiving top quality service, and completed the checks Mr. Kingsley asked you to do."

"I'm glad that's over." Stephen looked down at the box, but didn't open it. "I wish I had been wrong about Kira, though."

"She had quite a brilliant scam going. I'm impressed your friend was able to figure it out."

Stephen nodded. "If I hadn't sent Jason the picture of Kira at the volunteer event, we may have never connected her with the guy from Maroon Creek Inn. She was smart to work with someone at an unrelated resort. Stealing credit card numbers from her guests and exchanging them for ones from the other resort made it much harder to track. I can't believe Jason managed to get that information out of her.

"Did you know Snowcap had seventy-three guests report suspicious activity on their credit cards after staying at the lodge? Inquiries were made with the staff..."

"But since Kira wasn't making the charges, there was no way to connect her to them," Lizzie jumped in.

Stephen nodded. "Who knows how long she could have continued."

"I know Mr. Kingsley was happy to find out she was the only bad employee in the list he gave you. Even if she wasn't costing the hotel money now, she could've stepped up her stealing in the future."

"I didn't like turning her in, but I did kind of enjoy the process. I wonder, as MySpace grows in popularity, if companies might start using it to monitor their employees."

"I still don't understand the allure of putting personal information out for the whole world to see. If I have something I want to share, I'll pick up the phone or send an email."

Stephen shrugged. "I can see pros and cons for it. When I went to the page for Michelle's band, there was a list of her upcoming shows and comments from hundreds of people. That has to be encouraging to her and her bandmates."

"It probably is, and using the site for business may be a good thing. Maybe the hotel should consider creating a page."

Stephen chuckled. "Who do you think would get the job of keeping it updated? You know it won't be Jonathan or the GM."

Lizzie grimaced. "You're right, it would end up being me. Let's not mention the idea to anyone. Now open your present."

Stephen pulled at the ribbon and removed the box lid. Inside he found a sleek business card holder, engraved with his name and the title Ace Detective. He picked up the case and opened it, surprised to find it was already filled with cards.

He looked up at Lizzie. "These say Assistant Manager."

She gave him an innocent bat of her eyelashes. "Did I forget to mention the promotion?"

"Are you serious?"

"Completely. I actually had to beg Mr. Kingsley to let me keep you here. He wants you to move to HR." Lizzie held up her hand when Stephen started to speak and he leaned back in his chair, questions beating against the back of his throat.

"The HR position will still be available for you, if you want it, once Tammy gets back and I don't have to split my attention so much."

"What if I want to stay here? Will I still be assistant manager when Tammy gets back?"

"Yes, I convinced the GM that we need more leadership down here and you are the best candidate. You would be great in HR too, though, so I want you to think about what is best for you."

Stephen removed his glasses and pulled his polishing cloth from his pocket. He rubbed the lenses for several minutes, then held them up to the light and rubbed some more. "Do you know anything about the HR position?"

Lizzie reached into her purse and pulled out a manila envelope. "I haven't looked at it. Cynthia said if you have any questions you could give her a call."

Stephen took the envelope. "I'll look it over tonight."

"Take your time. Like I said, I have you until things get back to normal here."

"Normal? Have we had a normal day since I started?"

Lizzie tilted her head. "There was that one day in January."

Stephen laughed. "Normal is highly overrated anyway."

"I better get busy if I'm going to get out of here on time. Ian and I are planning to choose a venue for the wedding tonight."

"So you finally settled on a date?"

"Assuming we can agree on a venue that is available, December 17."

"A week before Christmas? Are you crazy?"

"I would have preferred something in October or early November, but it's a date that works for his parents as well as for Ron and Emma."

"You aren't considering the hotel as one of your venues, are you?"

"No, you were right. I wouldn't be able to stop checking on things long enough to be the bride. Ian thinks we should hire a wedding planner, but I want to keep it simple. I want to get married in a church, but ours is way too big. I'm looking for something small and charming with someplace nearby for the reception. You have any ideas?"

"Have you considered something in St. Augustine?"

"No, but that's not a bad idea. Maybe you could work some of your sleuthing magic and get me a list of possibilities?"

Stephen scooted his chair closer to his desk and reached for the keyboard. "I'll see what I can find. You take care of whatever is on your schedule today. Jessica should be in soon and I can have her get the arrival packets ready."

Lizzie placed a hand on his shoulder. "I don't know what I'll do without you."

Stephen stopped typing and looked up at Lizzie. He saw pride in her eyes and remembered how unsure of himself he'd been when she'd first taken him under her wing, training him during the tumultuous summer. He was no longer the trembling boy afraid to approach Chef Gustave or tell a guest "no". He hadn't been uncomfortable in the role of boss that he'd been thrown into when Lizzie had been away. He realized he'd loved every minute of the past year, but was there anything left for him to learn in this role?

"You sound like I've already made a decision to take the HR job."

"I'll understand if you do. You've come a long way in a short time and I'm incredibly proud of you." She squeezed his shoulder. "Now get to work."

He smiled. "Yes, ma'am."

His fingers now flew over the keyboard, keen to embark on his next mission.

Acknowledgements

Continuing the story of Lizzie, Ian, Jeffrey, Stephen, and Michelle has been a blast. As always, I have to thank my parents, Mike and Alta, who have encouraged me and supported me through all of the ups and downs of the writing process. Thanks to Jeff Gower, retired fire captain, for his guidance in writing Jeffrey's accident and the actions of the first responders. Thank you to Gary Bishop for helping me understand more of the construction process.

I have some of the best beta-readers, Gail, DiVoran, Jeanette, Sharon, and Pam. Thank you for finding the holes and making sure all of the details are in order. A special thanks to my editor, Clive Johnson. Your feedback makes me a better writer and I look forward to working with you more in the future. Most of all, I thank God for the inspiration and desire to follow this writing path.

I appreciate all of the support I've received from my readers and hope you enjoyed this newest installment of the *Seasons of Faith*. Stay tuned for more details on the wedding in *Christmas Vow*. You can check out some ideas Lizzie has for the wedding on Pinterest.

If you would like to learn more about my books please become a fan of my Facebook page at:

http://www.facebook.com/AuthorRebekahLyn

You can also follow me on Twitter @RebekahLyn1, or visit my website, RebekahLynBooks.com. If you love food and would like to find some of the recipes from my books check out my blog at:

http://www.rebekahlynskitchen.wordpress.com